Let's Connect!

Thank you for taking time to read this story! I pray you enjoy it and that you will continue to follow my work as a self-published author who desires to change the world through writing! Please leave a review on Amazon at the link below, they mean everything and is always appreciated!

God Bless,
Author Aundrya Schnel

www.amazon.com/author/aundryaschnel
www.amazon.com/author/aundryatheauthor

Podcast – When Silence Breaks

Impact Writing LLC
impactwritingllc.square.site

TRIBUTE

My Late Mother

Minister Linda Darlene Collins-Richardson
July 4, 1959 - June 19, 2005

My Late Grandmother

Mother Harriett Richardson
October 10, 1931 - February 4, 2017

*Whosoever hateth his brother is a
MURDERER; and ye know that no murderer
hath eternal life abiding in him.*

I John 3:15 (KJV)

INTRODUCTION

"Hey son, I'm sorry I'm late. That meeting I had ran a little long. Are you okay?"

"You're fine, Grandpa! Yes, I'm okay. I just wanted us to talk about something important..."

"Oh, is that why you asked me to meet you at the park?"

"Yeah, I just wanted to be in a peaceful spot because what I have to ask you is difficult. But I feel like I need to do it."

"Well, it sounds pretty serious. I'm listening, what do you want to ask me?"

"Grandpa, you know how much I love you, right?"

"Of course!"

"You know I thank God for you and I appreciate you for everything you've done to take care of me over the years."

"Yes, I know..."

"I've been wanting to know where I came from for years. I never brought it up before now because I didn't want you to think I didn't love you or that I didn't appreciate you because I do!"

"I know you do..."

"So, I hope you can understand why I want to talk about this. I have a son now and when it dawned on me that I can't tell him anything about his father's history outside of you and the church, it made me want to get those answers. You understand that right, Grandpa?"

"Yes, I understand. I knew you would want to know one day, so I'm not surprised..."

"So, is it that painful?"

"What do you mean?"

"I mean, the fact that you've never tried telling me anything about my parents made me wonder if something bad happened..."

"Yes, a lot of things happened around the time you were born and yes, it is hard to talk about..."

"Grandpa, I'm not here to make you uncomfortable and if you don't want me to know it all, I'm okay with that. But can you tell me something? Just something that I can have for myself and something that I can tell my son about!"

"That's fair. I guess I do owe you that much..."

"Anything you share would be great, I promise..."

"This might be easier if you ask me questions and I answer them for you. Is that okay?"

"Yes, I have some right here!"

"You just happened to have those with you?"

"Well, I wrote these down when I was twelve and saved them all these years..."

"Wow! I don't know what to say. But go ahead son, I'm all ears..."

"What can you tell me about my biological mother and father?"

"Your mother was my oldest daughter and her name was Shannon..."

"Can I know her whole name?"

"Sure. Her name was Shannon Michele Montgomery."

"Wow, that's a beautiful name. What happened to her? How come I never met her?"

"Shannon had a lot of complications during her pregnancy, we almost lost you."

"What? Grandpa, I almost died while I was in the womb?"

"Yeah, you did. No one was more scared than I was. But the doctors were able to help your mom which was what kept you alive..."

"So what happened to my mom? How come I've never seen her before?"

"She had a heart attack a few minutes after you were born. The doctors tried saving her but it didn't work and she died..."

"Oh my God, that's terrible. I'm sorry, Grandpa. I know that has to be hard losing your first born and all..."

"Yeah, it was. But I still had you and I was happy about that more than anything."

"How come I took your last name instead of my father's last name?"

"Shannon unfortunately didn't know who your father was when we asked her about it."

"Are you serious? I'm not trying to be disrespectful but are you saying my mom got around? I mean, she was the preacher's daughter!"

"It's complicated..."

"Okay, I'll let it go. So who's idea was it to name me?"

"It was mine. I know I should have told you this before but I actually named you after my father, who is your great grandfather."

"Wow! Grandpa, I never knew that! His name was Jameson too?"

"Yeah, it was but he went by *James*. He was a pastor too before he passed away."

"Wow, it's an honor to be named after him. Do you think he would be proud of me if he was alive?"

"Most definitely! He would be very proud!

"How old was my mom when she got pregnant with me?"
"Your mom was seventeen when she found she was pregnant with you..."
"Wow, she was so young..."
"Yeah and like I said, she said she didn't know who the father was so we didn't know..."
"When you say *"we,"* you mean you and Grandma?"
"Yes..."
"You've never talked about her either. I mean, can I ask about her too?"
"I don't have much to say, our marriage didn't work out. She wanted a divorce so I gave it to her. She left and I never saw her again..."
"That's it?"
"Yeah, pretty much..."
"Is it too much for you to tell me her name?"
"Her name was Natalie Patrice Hampton. We finalized our divorce back then and that was it. I never saw her again."
"Okay, I got it. Grandpa, thank you. Thank you for answering my questions and I can see why this wasn't easy for you."
"You're welcome, anything for you. So is that all you wanted to know?"
"I guess my last question was if I had any aunts or uncles, or was my mom an only child?"
"She was an only child..."
"What about any of my other relatives?"
"Natalie's parents disowned her for wanting to be with me and her sisters and brothers turned against her too so they wouldn't be on bad terms with their

parents. I know that Natalie had two sisters and two brothers so, it was five of them altogether. But we never saw them again once Natalie chose to be with me."
"Do you know why they didn't think you were good enough? I mean, you were the pastor's son."
"Natalie's parents were pastors too and her father had some issue with my father from way back in the day. It had something to do with an ordination, I forget the details."
"Are you serious? They held a grudge that long?"
"Yeah, leader wounds are the most dangerous..."
"What does that mean?"
"You will find out soon enough, trust me..."
"Do you have any brothers and sisters?"
"I have brothers. One was older and one was younger. The youngest one died when we were kids after getting hit by a car. The older one went to prison for murder when he was nineteen, I was 17-years-old at the time. He was sentenced to life in prison and I never saw or talked to him again. He's probably dead by now and my parents both died a year apart from each other. My father left his church for me to run and that's how I ended up becoming a pastor."
"Wow, that is big. Did you know that his will was set up that way?"
"He wasn't going to tell me because he knew I was running from my call to be a pastor. But my mom, your great grandmother, Ayda told me."
"I got it. What were your brothers' names?"

"The youngest one who died was named Darnell Lorenzo Mongtomery and my older brother's name is Derrick Elgin Montgomery, but we called him Ricky."

"Got it. Thank you again, Grandpa for telling me all of this. This helps me a lot. I don't feel as lost anymore."

"You felt lost?"

"Yeah, sort of. I mean, watching the other kids with their parents and not knowing mine was hard at times..."

"I did my best to fill that void for you, but I get it. I know it's not the same..."

"Not all the time but like I said, I appreciate you for everything you've ever done for me. I wouldn't be where I am without you."

"Well, that means a lot coming from you. Just know that I love you and I trust you with everything I have."

"I love you too, Grandpa. Can I ask you one more thing?"

"Of course..."

"How did you heal your wounds?"

"What are you talking about?"

"Well you said leader wounds are the most intense, right? I mean, you went through all of this pain and trauma in your life before and after you started pastoring. How did you heal from it?"

"I just prayed about it and moved on, that's all I could do..."

"You never talked about how you were feeling?"

"If you're asking if I went to counseling, no, I didn't go to counseling..."

"I had God and that was enough..."

"Grandpa, I know you taught me to trust God for everything and I do. But trauma is trauma and wounds are wounds. I just don't want you to have these wounds while you lead God's people."
"I appreciate your concern but I'm fine, I promise. I've been preaching longer than you've been alive so I promise you, I got it..."
"Are you sure?"
"I'm positive! No wound has ever stopped me and it never will..."

MURDER IN THE PEWS
Leader Wounds

TWO YEARS LATER

31-year-old, Pastor Jameson Montgomery, Sr. lives in Gainesville, Florida with his wife, Alexis, their 5-year-old son, Jameson *"Isaiah"* and their 2-year-old identical twin daughters, Destiny and Victoria. Jameson had grown up with his grandfather, Pastor Damian Montgomery since he was first born. Even though he didn't have a typical family dynamic with two parents and siblings in the home, Jameson always felt that he had a pretty stable upbringing and he never felt neglected by his grandfather, even though he was busy with the church. Jameson was taught about God and the Bible from an early age and when Jameson was 12-years-old, he gave his life to the Lord and a year later, Damian allowed Jameson opportunities to preach and teach in the pulpit. Jameson did it willingly not knowing that it would one day lead to him taking over his grandfather's church after his sudden passing of what was ruled as a heart attack.

After Damian's death, Jameson assumed that his grandfather's assistant pastor would take over as pastor until the day they gathered for reading of the will and realized that Damian wanted Jameson to take over as the senior pastor of his church once he passed away. Jameson was just as shocked as the rest of them because Damian never told Jameson that he intended on leaving him to run the church in his place once he was gone. But Damian's assistant pastor, Cole Scott, III didn't see it that way. He was not only angry that Damian didn't assign him as the pastor but he accused Jameson of withholding that information on purpose, when the truth was,

Jameson really had no idea. The news caused an unexpected divide in the church when Cole decided to leave the ministry, start his own church and take several of the members with him. There weren't a lot of people that attended as it was, so losing them so suddenly left Jameson to practically start over again with who he had left. Jameson was only 29-years-old at the time when all of this took place and even though he had no experience leading an entire congregation by himself, he had a lot of knowledge on how to do it from the things his grandfather taught him. The training that Jameson remembered his grandfather taking him through when he was younger made sense now that he was stepping into a role he didn't think he would ever walk in.

After the split, the only people that were only a select few left at the church including Jameson's two best friends, Nick and Ethan who he ordained to become his new assistant pastors. Everyone else was gone. Jameson met with the group he had left and decided to put some changes into place as they prepared to start over. With all of their help, they were able to do promotional ads inviting people to their ministry for service and announcing Jameson as the new pastor of their ministry, Christ Believers Church. Some suggested changing the name of the church but Jameson wanted to keep his grandfather's legacy alive by keeping it the same, even though a lot of changes were being made to the way things were done. Within three months of them advertising the ministry on social media, the local radio stations and paying for a commercial, the ministry began to grow and expand in record time. People were coming to gather from everywhere and it blew Jameson's mind because he wasn't expecting the turnaround to happen so quickly..

It has now been two years and the ministry continues to thrive in a way it never had before and Jameson was thankful because his true desire was to serve the people and teach them about the love of God. Jameson would soon learn that growth of his ministry was deeper than good advertisement, but it was as a result of the hold that was keeping the church in a state of bondage and even fear when Damian was still alive and doing things his way. Jameson was glad that he and his grandfather were able to talk and that Damian told him about his parents because it gave him closure. But, Jameson would soon learn that there was more to his grandfather's than what Damian chose to share with him, and the truth would leave Jameson with the chance to see freedom take place in the lives of people who have suffered at the wounds of the leaders that came before him.

It was another Saturday afternoon for Jameson who was at Alexis' parents' house celebrating Destiny and Victoria's second birthday today with their other family and members from the church. Jameson met Alexis when they were in fifth grade and they have been inseparable ever since. They went to the same schools and even attended college together in Atlanta with Jameson at Morehouse and Alexis at Spelman. Alexis' parents are doctors, so it didn't surprise him when Alexis studied medicine and made her career at one of the top pharmacies in the state. Jameson studied Accounting and Business, and he makes his living as a real estate agent who also flips houses on the side in addition to what he does as a pastor. Jameson always had a close relationship with Alexis' parents, but he and Alexis never understood the unspoken tension between Alexis' parents and Jameson's grandfather. Damian never treated Alexis poorly at all and he accepted her when Jameson and Alexis started dating, but neither of them could understand what was going on between them. They tried hiding it and most people didn't notice it, but Alexis and Jameson knew something was off with their interaction.

The tension between them became even more strange five years ago when Alexis' father, Dr. Robert *"Bobby"* Carrington, Sr. was rushed to the hospital with life threatening injuries after being stabbed in the stomach. Bobby was well known and respected in their community, so no one could understand why someone would want to hurt him. Jameson remembers how strange Damian started acting when it was time for them to go visit Bobby in the hospital. He acted as if he didn't want to go at first by saying he had other things to do, but he eventually changed his mind. Jameson wanted to be there for Alexis who was extremely worried along with the rest of her family, so he didn't question him about it. Bobby survived his injuries and made a full recovery after his surgery. The police investigated, but were never able to find out who stabbed Bobby since he explained not being able to see the face of the person who hurt him.

He told them the stabbing happened in the parking deck as he was leaving work late one night and the police thought they would be able to get surveillance footage of what took place. But unfortunately, the cameras in the deck where Bobby's car was parked were not working that week so there was no footage to turn into the police, at least that's what they were told. A couple of hours after the party started, Jameson's daughters had fallen asleep and he decided to talk to Bobby alone outback near the pool while everyone else continued talking inside the house.

It's been two years since Jameson lost his grandfather after he suffered a massive heart attack. Ever since, Jameson has found himself still feeling incomplete about his life even though Damian answered all of his questions when they were at the park that day. He can't help but wonder if there is more to his past than what his grandfather shared, but he didn't want to think about that too much because he didn't want it to seem as if he was accusing his own grandfather of lying to him. But what Jameson didn't realize is that what he was feeling wasn't wrong, it was the truth. His grandfather didn't tell him everything and many of the things he did share were lies to cover the truth, truth that would expose him in the worst way possible if it were ever revealed.

"This party turned out pretty nice, don't you think?" Bobby asked as the two of them sat down and continued drinking their wine.

"Yeah, it did. The ladies did a great job decorating for it, I really appreciate it and my daughters loved it!" Jameson replied as Bobby smiled a little and nodded.

"Nothing's too good for my granddaughters, they will always have the best from us." Bobby said as Jameson agreed with him.

"I feel the same way, Isaiah too. We're doing well for ourselves so our kids can have the best lives possible." Jameson told him as Bobby nodded.

"So, what's going on with you? You looked bothered when you said you wanted to talk. Is everything okay?" Bobby asked as Jameson sighed and paused for a moment before responding.

"Dad, I don't know how to say this because I know it will sound crazy." Jameson said.

"Nothing you tell me is crazy, Jameson. Just tell me what's on your mind." Bobby replied.

"I thought having my grandfather tell me where I came from was going to help fill a void of not knowing all these years and at first, it helped. But after my grandfather died, I started feeling that emptiness again. It's like I'm still without answers and I don't know why I feel that way! I mean, I'm sure my grandfather told me everything he knew, right?" Jameson asked as Bobby took another sip of his wine before responding.

"I mean, I'm sure he did. So, you asked Damian about your parents?" he asked.

"Yeah..."

"I didn't know that. When did you ask him?" Bobby asked.

"Two years ago. Literally a couple of months before he died and before Alexis and I found out she was pregnant again. I met him at Westside Park one day to ask questions I had been wanting to know since I was a kid." Jameson said.

"Wow, he let you ask? I mean, what did he tell you?" Bobby asked.

"He said that my mom had me when she was a teenager and that she didn't know who my father was, so, that's why I was named after my great grandfather." Jameson said as he watched Bobby's odd reaction to what he was saying.

"Did he tell you where your mom was?" Bobby asked.

"Yeah, he told me my mom died of a heart attack minutes after giving birth to me. He told me that my grandmother left him and that he never saw her again after their divorce." Jameson said as Bobby shook his head in disbelief. "What is it?"

"Nothing, I'm just saddened to hear that. I know you've probably wanted to meet your grandmother and your mother all these years. I mean, it sounds like Damian told you what you wanted to know. What do you feel like is still missing, Jameson?" Bobby asked as Jameson took a moment to think before responding.

"I honestly don't know, but I feel this very strongly and the more I try to ignore it, the harder it is. I'm convinced that there's more to my past that I know nothing about and I don't know where to begin to get answers now that my grandfather is not alive. That's sort of why I wanted to talk to you." Jameson said as Bobby's expression changed.

"You wanted to talk to me? I mean, you know you can tell me anything but I don't have any answers for you." Bobby said.

"I know, it's not really about that. It's about something else that I noticed from the first time you and my grandfather met, but I never said anything about it before now." Jameson said.

"What's that?" Bobby asked, curiously.

"Alexis sort of wondered about this too but I don't think she thought about it as much as I did. It seemed like you and my grandfather had this weird, unspoken tension between the two of you. You tried not to show it but I sense something wasn't right with the two of you. You hardly ever talked to each other, even when we were having family gatherings." Jameson said.

"Oh, is that what you thought? I mean, I never had that kind of connection with your grandfather but there was no tension. We were okay." Bobby replied.

"Are you sure? I mean, I'll never forget the way he reacted when I told him we had to rush to the hospital after you got stabbed. He acted like he didn't want to go see you which made no sense. My grandfather always had a heart of compassion for the sick and I didn't think you would be any different, but he literally almost decided not to go. I had to almost beg him. I didn't confront him about it, but I always wondered why he responded that way." Jameson said as Bobby sighed and shrugged his shoulders.

"Yeah Jameson, I'm not sure why he responded that way." Bobby said as Jameson nodded and paused for a moment before responding.

"Dad, can I ask you something?" Jameson asked.

"Of course!"

"You didn't know my grandfather prior to meeting him when Alexis and I were kids did you?" Jameson asked.

"I mean, he looks like someone I knew back in the day when I was young. But no, I didn't know Damian beforehand." Bobby said.

After their conversation, Jameson and Bobby went back inside the house to rejoin everyone at his daughters' birthday party. Jameson didn't know why he was feeling the way he did, but he couldn't help but wonder if Bobby was telling him the truth. As he drove home with his wife and children, he couldn't stop thinking about the way he was feeling. Even though Alexis kept asking him if he was okay, he didn't tell her what he was thinking about because he didn't know how she would respond with what he would end up saying about her father. Jameson counted it an honor when he asked Bobby for his blessing before asking Alexis to marry him and he told Jameson he could call him "*Dad.*" It was one of the best feelings he ever felt and it made their bond even closer. It was why the thought of Bobby lying to him was really making him worry. Jameson has always been able to trust Bobby and now that his grandfather was no longer alive, he didn't know how he would feel if Bobby ever did anything to betray his trust. Sunday at church, Nick preached which was a sigh of relief for Jameson, even though Nick was scheduled to speak today a month ago. Nick taught a great message and a large number of people came to the altar for prayer and ten of them decided to join the church. Seeing new people added to the ministry always made Jameson happy and he did his best to focus on that so he wouldn't remain distracted about his conversation with Bobby and all of his other concerns.

When service was over, Alexis' parents, Bobby and Crystal came by to pick up their children and watch them at their house until Jameson and Alexis finished up with everything at the church. Nick's message was about being healed from past hurt and Jameson was overwhelmed by the number of people he and Alexis talked to today who had been through past hurt, rejection and even levels of trauma with former pastors. Some of them had incidents they were still dealing with from their childhood. The most unique detail about each of the people they spoke to was they were all former ministers, elders, prophets and even pastors. Hearing their stories made Jameson remember something that his grandfather said to him two years ago when they talked that day in the park. Damian told Jameson that leader wounds were the most dangerous. Jameson remembered asking him what that meant and Damian told him that he would one day find out what it meant for himself, and he was right. Jameson knew exactly what his grandfather meant and he was able to see first hand how important it was for leaders to heal before they attempt to lead others, not knowing that he would one day see what happened as a result of the wounds that his grandfather was never healed from prior to his death. After the people left to go home, it was late in the afternoon and everyone was exhausted. Jameson quickly gathered his leader and other staff to speak with them briefly before they went home. Jameson encouraged everyone to do a daily check of their heart, their mind and their emotions. If they were dealing with any pain or hurt from their past in any way, Jameson did not want them to be afraid to address and do what was necessary to heal from it. Later that evening, when Jameson and Alexis were finally at home with their children, they decided to sit on the back patio to talk after watching each of their children fall asleep in their rooms.

"Baby, wasn't today awesome? I mean, every week is great but today was powerful! Maybe we should let Nick teach more often if he's going to draw this kind of response." Alexis said as she and Jameson both started laughing.

"Now you know, Nick will never go for that. He only teaches when I ask him to do it. He has no problem letting me preach every week. But I push him at times for reasons like what happened today, and I do the same with Ethan. We've been friends for a long time and I know what they both carry so I push them in it. Babe, you don't think I came off crazy with what I said to everyone in our briefing after church today do you?" Jameson asked.

"Oh no, of course not. What you said was great and I think everyone received what you told them." Alexis replied as Jameson sighed and nodded before leaning over to kiss his wife on her forehead.

"Thank you, baby, I appreciate it." Jameson said as he and Alexis smiled at each other.

"You're welcome!"

"Babe, can I ask you something?" Jameson asked.

"Of course! What is it?" Alexis asked, curiously as Jameson sighed before responding.

"This may sound like an odd question but I promise, I'm asking for a reason. Babe, have your parents ever told you about how they grew up or how they got together as a couple?" Jameson asked as Alexis nodded.

"Yeah, they told us. But wait, I thought I told you what they said." Alexis said.

"No, I don't remember you doing that and I never thought to ask. What did they tell you?" Jameson asked.

"Well, it was pretty shocking to hear. So, you know my parents were born and raised in Chicago. Their parents were actively involved in church so they went to church every week growing up, it was all they knew!" Alexis replied as Jameson reacted to what she told him.

"Are you serious? Your parents grew up in the church? But, they're so against it now. I mean, the only time they came to church was when our son was christened." Jameson said.

"Yeah, I said the same thing and I asked them why was it that we never grew up going to church like they did. I mean, I didn't start attending church like that until I met you and that was only on occasion." Alexis said.

"Exactly. So, what did they say?" Jameson asked.

"Baby, their story is one for the books for real. My parents told us that at one point they were training to become ministers and everything." Alexis said.

"Are you serious? They were going through training too? Did they say what church it was?" Jameson asked.

"No, they never said which church. Just that it was where their parents went in Chicago at the time. I asked them why they never became ministers and they said it was because my mom found out she was pregnant with me. My parents weren't married, they were both fresh out of high school at that point and everyone including their parents gave them a hard time for it." Alexis said.

"Is that why you never saw your grandparents?" Jameson asked as Alexis nodded.

"Yeah, that's why. Mom said the church acted like they had done the worst thing possible and even said that they would be cursed for getting pregnant.

They were kicked out of the church and their parents did nothing to support them. They were up to be ordained soon and they knew it wouldn't happen if they tried standing by their side, so they sided with the pastor's decision to kick them out. My parents had just been accepted into school at the University of Florida and they left Chicago, came here for school and never looked back." Alexis said.

"Are you serious? So they still went to school even with your mom being pregnant with you?" Jameson asked.

"Yeah, they did and they went through so much between school, the pregnancy and then finding somewhere to stay on their budget once I was born because they couldn't bring a baby into the dorms." Alexis said.

"That is one of the wildest stories I have ever heard. So how did they do it?" Jameson asked.

"A lady who worked on campus felt bad for them and when they left the dorm, she offered them a place to stay at a property she owned not far from the campus. They moved in, continued school and even got jobs so they could take care of me, my brother who was born two years later and pay rent to the lady who was helping them. They had scholarships to pay for the tuition and they just pushed through until they both finished, went to medical school and became doctors." Alexis said as Jameson shook his head in disbelief.

"Wow, what a story. I'm surprised they don't talk more about it. What ever happened to the woman who helped them? Did they say?" Jameson asked.

"Yeah, she died in her sleep not long after my mom found out she was pregnant with Jason. She left the house to them so they fixed it up and turned it into a rental property for people in need of housing." Alexis said.

"Wow, that is amazing. I'm shocked right now." Jameson said.

"Why did you want me to tell you about that, Jameson?" Alexis asked.

"I'm just trying to connect some dots for myself about my life." Jameson replied.

"You are? I thought Grandpa Damian answered your questions before he died like you told me." Alexis said.

"He did and I was good with it until he passed away. I started feeling uneasy again, almost like there's more to what he said." Jameson told her as she needed.

"I can understand you feeling that way but what does my parents have to do with it?" Alexis asked, concerned.

"I don't know. But I asked you about their background because of the weird tension we used to notice between your father and my grandfather. Don't you remember?" Jameson asked.

"Yeah, but I didn't think much of it. You still think there's something to it?" Alexis asked.

"Yeah, I do. I can't help but wonder if my grandfather and your dad knew each other and now that you've told me that your parents grew up in Chicago, it's really making me wonder. Think about it, my mother was born and raised in Chicago too, and she was seventeen when she had me, Alexis! Only like a year or two younger than your parents. What if they knew each other? What if they were in my grandfather's church back when he was pastor in Chicago." Jameson said.

"What? Baby, that is a stretch. I mean, yes it's ironic that our parents are from the same city but Chicago is huge, and I just don't believe your grandfather would have done something like what my parents described. Kicking two of their young people out of the church because they got pregnant? That doesn't sound like him at all! I mean, think about Nick and Ethan. He didn't hound them when they both had kids out of wedlock." Alexis said as Jameson nodded and paused for a moment before responding.

"That's true, he didn't. He helped them out. I guess I'm losing it." Jameson replied.

"No baby, you're okay. You just want answers and I get that. But what answers do you think you still need at this point? I mean, are you wanting to see if your grandmother is still alive?" Alexis asked.

"That's part of it, I want answers, period. I'm not saying my grandfather lied to me, but there's more and I just wish I knew where to begin." Jameson said as Alexis sat next to him in their bed and thought for a moment.

"How do you feel about hiring a private investigator to help you? I mean, you can take the names that your grandfather gave you and see what they can connect from it." Alexis said as Jameson nodded.

"That's not a bad idea, I'll look into one. Thank you." Jameson said as they kissed each other.

"You're welcome. If there's anything left for you to find out, an investigator will find it. I guess my only question is, are you ready for the answers?" Alexis asked as Jameson's expression changed.

"What do you mean?" he asked.

"I mean, sometimes when we go looking for answers to things we don't know, we at times get answers we weren't prepared for." Alexis said.

"Yeah, I didn't think about that either. I guess it's the risk I'm willing to take because I definitely want to make sure I know everything there is to know about my history and where I came from." Jameson replied.

"Well, I'll be here every step of the way and whatever I can do to help you, I will." Alexis said as she and Jameson hugged and kissed each other.

"I love you, Alexis Montgomery!" Jameson said as she started smiling.

"I love you too, Jameson Montgomery!"

The next morning, after Alexis left for work at the pharmacy and Jameson dropped their children off with their parents, he drove to his office at the church to get some work done and to start looking up information on a good private investigator he could consider hiring. Jameson was tempted to ask Bobby about he and his wife's experience in the church when they got pregnant before they were married at such young ages. Bobby was on a business call when he came over so he decided not to ask him about it now, but he knew it would be something he would want to talk about later. Even though Jameson knew Alexis was right about what she said, he couldn't help but wonder if his own suspicions were right about Bobby and his grandfather knowing each other. Time would only tell if what Jameson was suspecting would turn out to be true. When Jameson arrived at his office, he noticed the church's secretary, Brittany was not at her desk and didn't appear that she had been at work all morning. Jameson walked over to sit at his desk so he could call Brittany and see where she was, but before he could do it, his accountant, Dwayne, came to the door and knocked.

"Hey Pastor, are you busy?" Dwayne asked as Jameson sat the phone back on the hook.

"Hey Dwayne, I just got here, actually. I was about to call Brittany to see where she was. Have you seen her this morning? She didn't call me to say she wasn't coming in." Jameson said, concerned as he wondered why she wasn't at her desk.

"That's actually what I came to talk to you about. We have a situation on our hands and I figured it was best that Brittany went home until I was able to talk to you about it." Dwayne said Jameson's expression changed.

"What? Wait a minute, Dwayne. You sent my secretary home without calling me first? I hope you had a good reason for it, Dwayne." Jameson said, sternly as Dwyane nodded and sat at Jameson's desk.

"Yes sir, I did. I found something in the church's finances that I didn't realize was there before now." Dwayne said.

"What is it and what does it have to do with you sending Brittany home?" Jameson asked as Dwayne handed a file folder full of bank statements to Jameson to look at.

"I made copies so you could see it for yourself because I knew you wouldn't believe me otherwise. Pastor Montgomery was sending five thousand dollars from a private account into Brittany's checking account twice a month. I traced it back and he had been doing it for the last five years, since Brittany was sixteen and the payments were still automatically going to her account today. Last payment was made last week. I knew something was off and I couldn't figure it out, now I see it." Dwayne said as Jameson shook his head.

"This doesn't make any sense to me at all. Why would my grandfather be sending this much money to her and why has he been doing it since she was a minor? Did you talk to Brittany before you sent her home?" Jameson asked, confused about what was going on.

"Yes, I did and that's why I sent her home. It was either I send her home or slap the smirk off her face when I asked her about it." Dwayne said.

"What are you talking about, Dwayne? What did she say?" Jameson asked.

"Brittany said that she and Pastor Damian had been having sex since she was sixteen and he was paying her to keep quiet." Dwayne said as Jameson reacted to what he said.

"What? No way! No way! My grandfather wasn't like that!" Jameson said.

"Pastor, I get what you're saying but look at those statements. What else would he be sending that money to her for and why send it from a private account?" Dwayne said as Jameson leaned back in his seat and shook his head, still shocked about what Dwayne told him.

"I can't believe this..."

"There's one more thing. Brittany said that her 3-year-old son is Pastor Damian's. That's why she had been continuing to receive payments all this time." Dwayne said.

"What? He got her pregnant? No! No way! I don't believe any of this right now. He had to be sending her this money for some other reason!" Jameson replied, defensively.

"Pastor, c'mon now, you know he wouldn't be sending this much money to her just because." Dwayne said.

"How did she act when you confronted her? I mean, outside of the smirk. Did she threaten to tell anyone if we didn't keep paying her?" Jameson asked.

"Sort of. Before she walked out, she said if I didn't want you to get embarrassed, I better keep the payments coming. Then she handed me this." Dwayne said, handing another document to Jameson.

"What is it?" Jameson asked.

"Paternity test results. Pastor Damian had the kid tested and it says it's his." Dwayne replied as Jameson paused for a moment before responding.

"Did you tell Nick or Ethan about this yet?" Jameson asked.

"Not yet, Pastor. I wanted to wait and see what you wanted to do. I have some cousins who can handle her and that kid if you want, just say the word." Dwayne replied.

"No sir, please do not call your cousins about her! If she gets hurt and the police start snooping around, they're going to realize she was my grandfather's secretary and it won't take them long to find out that her son belongs to him. We have to do something else!' Jameson told him as Dwayne nodded.

"I got you, Pastor. You're not going to let her continue to be the secretary are you?" Dwayne asked as Jameson sighed and paused for a moment before responding.

"No, I can't do that. I can't let her work knowing she had a kid with my grandfather, who was the pastor of this church before he died and left it to me. Then I have to think about her parents. They left a year before my grandfather died and I never knew why. Do you know how livid they would be if they found out that their daughter had a baby by my grandfather?" Jameson asked as Dwayne shook his head and handed another document to him.

"I wanted to give you this in pieces." Dwayne said.

"What is this?" Jameson asked.

"Another statement. Around the time that Brittany's parents left the ministry, Pastor Damian wired one hundred grand to their bank account and I can almost guess why he did it." Dwayne said.

"Oh my God, they knew about this. They knew my grandfather was molesting their daughter and they took a payout instead of holding him accountable?" Jameson asked, disgusted.

"It looks that way based on how all of this is coming together. My guess is they found out what Pastor Damian did, they went to confront him and they probably threatened to expose him so he paid them off. They took the money and they left. But they didn't take Brittany with them, which makes me think that part of the agreement was for them to allow Brittany to remain at the church." Dwayne said.

"I can't believe what I'm hearing right now. My grandfather was a child molester?" Jameson asked, still in shock about what he was learning.

"It looks that way, Pastor. I'm sorry." Dwayne said, sadly as Jameson shook his head.

"I can't believe this right now. I know Brittany has been allowing herself to benefit from this, but I can't get over when this started, Dwayne. She was sixteen! Think about that! We both have little girls! Can you imagine finding out your baby girl has been getting molested by someone who was supposed to look out for her?" Jameson asked, enraged as Dwayne nodded.

"I don't know what I would do, I would probably kill the guy. So I get it. I'm sorry, I probably should not have sent Brittany home like that." Dwayne said as Jameson nodded.

"Don't worry about it, I know you panicked and I would have too. I don't want to push Brittany away but I have to figure out something to help her move on from this place. She just can't stay here. I'm going to go see her!" Jameson said as he quickly grabbed his things and started towards the door.

"You're going alone? I can come with you!" Dwayne said.

"Thanks, but I got it. I need you to stay here and make sure there's no other surprises that could ruin us with the church's money. Call me if you find anything. Can you do that?" Jameson asked as he and Dwayne slapped hands.

"Yes sir, I can handle that for you." Dwayne replied.

"Okay, cool. I'll be back in a couple of hours. If Nick or Ethan show up, don't tell them any of this yet. Just tell them I had to step out and I'll be back to meet with them later." Jameson said as Dwayne nodded in agreement.

Jameson quickly got into his truck and started driving towards the area where Brittany stayed. She lived in a nice house in one of Jacksonville's prominent suburbs and Jameson used to wonder how she was able to afford where she stayed with her entry level salary, but he never asked questions. He then remembered Alexis asking Brittany what else she did to make money because she was just as curious as he was about how she was affording such nice things with little income. Brittany told her that she worked part-time in sales, but Jameson now realized that wasn't the truth. She was being paid by his grandfather to keep quiet about their sexual relationship and the fact that she gave birth to their son.

Jameson was never a big fan of abortions, but he was surprised that his grandfather didn't go the route of paying for Brittany to get one instead of paying her off to raise their son without anyone knowing that he's the father. It just didn't make sense to him and he couldn't get over the fact that his grandfather would have been labeled a registered sex offender had he'd been arrested for what he did. When Jameson arrived at Brittany's house, he saw her car outside and decided to park on the street as he sat inside of his truck thinking about what he would say to Brittany when they talked. Brittany met Jameson outside on the front porch with her son as Jameson got out of his truck and started up the driveway towards them.]

"So, I guess you talked to Dwayne." Brittany said as Jameson sat at the table across from her while her son played near them with his toys.

"Yeah, I talked to him." Jameson replied as she nodded.

"Do you hate me now?" Brittany asked.

"No, I don't hate you. I'm just trying to process all of this. I mean, did you really start having sex with my grandfather when you were sixteen?" Jameson asked, disgusted.

"Yes, I did. But I didn't expect it to happen and I didn't really feel like I had a choice at the time." Brittany said as Jameson's expression changed.

"What do you mean? What happened?" Jameson asked.

"I was acting out a lot around that time of my life and my mom got overwhelmed and decided to talk to Pastor Damian about it. I wasn't there for the meeting so I don't really know what they said during the conversation. All I know is when my mom came out of the meeting one Sunday after church, she walked over to me and said that I was going to start doing some extra jobs for Pastor Damian at his house as a way for me to stay out of trouble." Brittany said as Jameson shook his head. "You want me to stop?"

"Only if you want to, Brittany. I'm not trying to make you uncomfortable by talking about this. But I can handle it if you can." Jameson replied as she nodded.

"I can handle it. I mean, you deserve to know the truth. I didn't think anything of it at first and the first Saturday I went to his house, that's where it happened." Brittany said.

"So, your mom didn't wait for you? She left you at my grandfather's house alone?" Jameson asked, surprised as Brittany nodded again.

"Yes, she left me alone while she went to the women's fellowship gatherings at one of the other leaders' houses. She would usually pick me up after a couple of hours or so." Brittany said.

"So he didn't have you do anything at the house except have sex with him, right?" Jameson asked.

"Yeah, pretty much. I was afraid at first, but Pastor Damian said he would pay me and he would even pay my mother's bills so we wouldn't struggle if I let it happen." Brittany told him as Jameson reacted to what she said.

"Wait, I assumed your mom didn't know about this. Evangelist Cora knew about this and didn't say anything?" Jameson asked.

"Yeah, she knew. After the first time it happened, I remember crying and I was in pain because I lost my virginity to Pastor Damian. I told my mom what happened when she picked me up and she just took a deep breath and said she was sorry but I had to help pay the bills and that was how I knew that all of this was arranged between the two of them." Brittany replied as Jameson shook his head.

"Brittany, I want to start by apologizing for how Dwayne went about things when he found the transfers my grandfather had sent you. He should not have sent you home like that and I checked him about it." Jameson said as Brittany nodded and smiled a little.

"It's okay, thank you for understanding where I was coming from. I appreciate it. I've never talked about it before now." Brittany replied.

"Are you serious, Brittany? You haven't been to counseling or anything?" Jameson asked as Brittany shook her head.

"No, I've just been dealing with it and I guess I didn't want the money to stop coming in so I kept it to myself." Brittany said.

"Well, I saw that she was still getting payments automatically sent to her too from my grandfather's private account and I've had Dwayne stop those payments immediately along with the ones that were being sent to you. I know money can't ever fix what happened to you, but will you accept this lump sum amount from the church?" Jameson asked, handing Brittany a check made out to her for $250,000.00.

"Oh my God! Are you serious?" Brittany asked, surprised.

"Yes, I'm serious. I wanted you to have that but please know it's not hush money." Jameson replied.

"It's not?" she asked.

"No, it's not hush money. I thought about everything when I was driving over here and even though I don't want the church in a scandal as a result of what my grandfather did, I won't stop you from reporting what happened or at least getting therapy if that's what you want to do. I'm just really sorry that all of this happened to you and that you felt the need to continue sleeping with him in secret." Jameson said as Brittany smiled and nodded.

"You've always been a good guy, I appreciate that. Thank you so much, Pastor Jameson." Brittany said, graciously as Jameson smiled a little and nodded.

"You're welcome..."

"I don't plan to expose what happened to anyone, I promise. But I will get counseling for myself so that I can make sure I'm okay with raising my son alone." Brittany said as Jameson nodded and glanced over at him.

"How old is he?" Jameson asked.

"Emanuel is 3-years-old now. His birthday was two months ago." Brittany said.

"His name is Emanuel?" Jameson asked.

"Yeah, it's his middle name. Pastor Damian insisted on him being named after him. So it's Damian Emanuel Montgomery." Brittany said as Jameson looked surprised.

"I can't believe he did that. So, he didn't give you a hard time when he realized you were pregnant?" Jameson asked.

"I thought he was going to but he didn't. When I told him I was pregnant, I was already open to an abortion but that wasn't what he wanted. He looked at me and told me long before I ever learned the sex of the baby that I was having a son." Brittany said.

"He said that?" Jameson asked.

"Yes, I was shocked too. He said he wanted me to name our son after him because he never got the chance to have a son of his own to carry his name. He told me that he only had daughters." Brittany said as

Jameson was caught off guard by Brittany's statement.

"Wait a minute, did you say daughters?" Jameson asked.

"Yeah..." she said.

"Did you mean to say that he told you he had one daughter?" Jameson asked as Brittany paused for a moment before responding.

"No, I didn't. Pastor Damian told me he had daughters. He never said how many but he definitely said he had them. Why do you ask?" Brittany asked as Jameson shook his head.

"My mother was his daughter and he told me that my mother was the only daughter he had." Jameson said as Brittany sat speechless for a moment.

"Oh wow, Pastor, I didn't know that. Yeah, he told me he had all girls and he was happy to finally have a son. Like I said, he never told me how many of them there were." Brittany said as Jameson nodded.

"Okay, thanks for letting me know that. Wow, this is crazy! I just thought of something else." Jameson said.

"What?" she asked.

"Your son is my uncle." Jameson replied as Brittany almost spit out her drink.

"Are you serious?" she asked.

"Yeah, I'm serious. My mother was my grandfather's daughter and he now has a son which means he's my uncle, and my kids are his great nephews and his great nieces." Jameson said as Brittany shook her head in disbelief.

"I can't believe that. Wow, I never thought about it like that. Well, I don't have a problem keeping this quiet." Brittany said.

"If you want to come back as my secretary, you can." Jameson told her.

"I appreciate it but it will be a lot to deal with now that Dwayne knows everything. He's not going to talk is he?" Brittany asked.

"No, he's not going to say anything. I already talked to him." Jameson said as Brittany nodded.

"I think it will be best if I just step down, I'm sorry to leave you without a secretary." Brittany told him.

"You don't have to apologize, you're fine. It won't take me long to find a replacement. I better get going, thanks for taking the time to talk to me at the last minute." Jameson said as the two of them stood up from the table.

"No problem, thanks for everything you've done too, I really do appreciate it." Brittany replied.

"You're welcome. Can I ask you one more thing before I go?" Jameson asked.

"Sure!"

"Did you ever hear my grandfather say anything else about his side of the family outside of what he told you about having more than one daughter?" Jameson asked as Brittany paused and thought for a moment.

"I remember one time, Pastor Damian and I got into an argument over something stupid when I was at his house one weekend. Even though he apologized later, I remember him saying how all women were the same and he said it was why he got rid of his wife when he had the chance." Brittany said as Jameson looked surprised.

"He said that?" Jameson asked.

"Yes, but I didn't know who he was referring to because he never said much to me about his past relationships." Brittany replied.

"Unless my grandfather lied about this too, he was only married once to my grandmother. He told me before he died that she left him and that she was the one who asked for the divorce." Jameson said.

"Oh wow, he said that to you? I don't think it happened like that based on what he said to me, Pastor Jameson. I think he left her, but I don't know why he did it." Brittany said as Jameson nodded.

"Thank you for telling me what you remembered, I appreciate it." Jameson said as Brittany smiled a little nodded.

Jameson left her house and drove to the storage location where he was keeping all of his grandfather's things of value. Brittany's statements to him about the things Damian said to her made him wonder even more if there was something that his grandfather didn't tell him before he died. Hearing that it was possible that he fathered more children was concerning because Damian always said he only had one daughter, which was Jameson's mother.

Damian's storage space was huge and he knew it would take him a while to search through everything, so, he reached out to Nick and Ethan and asked him to come to the storage area in fifteen minutes so they could help him. While Jameson did his best not to think about it too much, he couldn't help but wonder if there were other things that his grandfather wasn't honest with him about, and he was still very much disgusted by the fact that he had a son with the young woman that he molested and took advantage of. Jameson looked at Emanuel in shock at how much he resembled his son, Isaiah and as hard as it would be, he wanted to embrace him because he knows Emanuel is innocent and that he didn't ask for any of this. Moments after Jameson arrived at Damian's storage unit, Nick and Ethan showed up as he requested.

"Hey guys, thanks for coming on short notice. I appreciate it." Jameson said to them as they hugged and greeted each other.

"No problem man, you know we got you. You need us to help you move his stuff or something?" Nick asked as Jameson took a look at everything inside after opening the door.

"No, I'm not moving anything. I'm just going to take what I need once I find it. But that's what I need your help with." Jameson said as Nick and Ethan glanced at each other.

"You need us to help you find something in Pastor Damian's stuff?" Ethan asked.

"Yeah..."

"Okay Jay, we're down. But what do you need us to help you find, and are you okay? You look upset but you're trying to hide it. Of course you can't, we're your boys, we've known you too long." Ethan said as Jameson sighed and took a deep breath before responding.

"Yeah, it's been a really crazy morning and it's why I called you to meet me here. Let me ask you this, did you see Dwayne when you went to the church?" Jameson asked.

"Yeah, in passing. He was on his cell phone when he waved at us. Why?" Nick asked, concerned as Jameson nodded.

"Okay, good. He did what I said and didn't tell you anything." Jameson said.

"Tell us what, Jameson? What's going on?" Nick asked.

"You wouldn't believe me if I told you." Jameson replied as Nick and Ethan glanced at each other again, wondering what was going on.

"Bro, you can tell us anything. You know that! What's up?" Ethan asked as the three of them sat down on the bench outside the storage unit.

Jameson began to tell Ethan and Nick everything that he found out this morning from learning that Brittany had been in a sexual relationship with his grandfather since she was a teenager to finding out that her 3-year-old son is fathered by him, making him Jameson's uncle. As expected, Nick and Ethan were both in total shock to hear what Jameson was telling them and they felt bad for Jameson too, because they knew how hard all of this was on him. Jameson has been best friends with Ethan and Nick since they were in third grade and met for the first time when Nick and Ethan's mothers came to the church that summer for the backpack giveaway their church did every year for children in the community. Nick and Ethan's mothers weren't saved and had no interest in attending church, but they allowed Nick and Ethan to come to the events that the church would have for kids their age and that's how the three of them became close. Jameson didn't have to ask Nick or Ethan to keep this quiet from their mothers, because they still prayed daily for their mothers to get saved and come to the church. Information like this would give them another reason not to trust leaders in the church and that's not what they wanted, especially Jameson.

It's only been two years since Jameson took over as the senior pastor of his grandfather's church, and before today, he still questioned why he was chosen to take over when Pastor Scott had way more experience and technically would have been next in line for his position based on his current role as the assistant pastor. But Jameson is starting to see that none of this has happened by chance and his role in his grandfather's position comes with a mandate that will allow him to be used by God to see a shift that will not only reveal the things that have been hidden for too long, but will bring change into the lives of many, including him. Jameson will see that the answers to his questions will come to him in a way he would have never anticipated and the answers will not only give him clarity and a level of closure, but reconciliation will take place and what's been out of place all these years, will be realigned.

"Bro, I know you don't know her that well but my ex-girlfriend's cousin has several years of experience as an accountant and administrative assistant. She's no church goer, but if you need someone who can jump right into Brittany's role, she can do it. Just let me know." Nick said as Jameson nodded.

"Thank you, I'll let you know. Guys, I have one more thing to tell you and it's the main reason I asked you to meet me here." Jameson said as the three of them got up from where they were sitting and walked over to the entrance of the storage unit.

"Dang bro, there's more?" Ethan asked, surprised.

"A little bit. I came here after leaving Brittany's house because of something that she said when I was about to end our meeting. She said that my grandfather told her that he had all daughters." Jameson said.

"As in more than one daughter?" Ethan asked, surprised.

"Yes, more than one. He told Brittany to keep the baby when she told him she was pregnant because he had a feeling she was going to have a boy and he only had daughters and never had his son." Jameson said as Nick and Ethan reacted to what he said.

"So your mom's not his only child?" Nick asked in shock.

"I don't know for sure, but if he said that to Brittany, there's a good chance he had other daughters and I want to see if there's anything in here that would tell me the answer to that. So let's look for letters, pictures, birth certificates, anything! Anything that would indicate that he had more than one daughter." Jameson said as the three of them started searching.

"Okay man, we got you. Is that all we're looking for?" Nick asked as Jameson paused for a moment before responding.

"Let's look for my mom's death certificate too. If she died giving birth to me, there should be a death certificate." Jameson replied.

"Okay, got it. Jameson, what happens if we don't find a death certificate for your mom? I mean, it could have gotten lost, right?" Ethan asked.

"Yeah, that's possible. But it could also mean that she's still alive, and at this point, I want to be sure." Jameson said as Ethan and Nick agreed with him.

"Okay bro, we're here. We will do what we can to help you find the answers you're looking for." Ethan replied.

"Thanks, I appreciate it. Can you guys also keep your eyes open for Natalie Patrice Hampton?" Jameson asked as they started searching through Damian's things.

"Yeah, we can do that. Who is she?" Nick asked.

"My grandmother, according to what my grandfather told me. He said they got divorced when my mom was still really young and he said he never saw her again once she left home." Jameson said.

"You don't think that's true anymore either?" Nick asked.

"I'm not trying to accuse my grandfather of being a liar, I just want to double check everything he said. He said he never saw her again which could mean anything. I mean, what if she's still alive." Jameson said.

"I got it. If we find anything of hers or with her name on it, we will let you know. Have you told Alexis about all of this yet?" Nick asked.

"No, I haven't talked to my wife since we left for work this morning. But I plan to, and I also plan to do what she suggested about hiring a private investigator depending on what we find here today." Jameson said.

"Why did she suggest that? I mean, it's not a bad idea, I'm just curious." Ethan said.

"She suggested over the weekend after we came back from the twins' birthday party at her parents' house. I was asking her if her parents had ever told her anything about the way they grew up and I asked her how they met. I asked her this because there was always this weird vibe between her dad and my grandfather that I couldn't understand." Jameson said.

"Really? So, they didn't get along?" Ethan asked.

"I mean, they did, but it was like they only spoke to each other when they had to. The times I did see them in the same room, there was just this subtle tension that I always noticed, but I couldn't understand what it was. I mean, when Alexis' father got stabbed, I had to almost beg my grandfather to go to the hospital with me. It was crazy!" Jameson said.

"Are you serious? He's usually always going to help someone in need. Why would he hold back like that?" Nick asked, surprised.

"I have no idea and at the time, everything was happening so fast, I never did ask him what it was about." Jameson replied.

"So you never asked Pastor Damian about any of this at all?" Nick asked.

"No, I didn't ask and I wish I had. But I did try talking to Alexis' father about it at the party Saturday. I told him what I thought and I asked him straight out. I asked him if he and my grandfather knew each other." Jameson said.

"What did he say?" Ethan asked.

"He said my grandfather looked familiar, but he didn't know him prior to meeting when we were in elementary school." Jameson replied.

"Okay, do you believe him?" Nick asked as Jameson sighed and paused for a moment before responding.

"This may sound bad, but I don't believe him, and I don't even know why I feel that way. I mean, he's never lied to me before and I've always been able to trust him. But for some reason, I don't think he told me the truth about that. I think they did know each other." Jameson said.

"Did you tell Alexis?" Ethan asked.

"What? No way! I mean, I have no proof or any valid suspicion to be vocal about it. She would just get upset with me for not believing him and what good would that do if I don't have anything to say outside of the fact that I'm suspicious about it?" Jameson asked as Nick and Ethan nodded.

"Yeah, that makes sense. Well bro, if it's the truth, it will come out one way or the other. That goes for everything else you're trying to find. Things can only remain in the dark for so long." Ethan said as Jameson nodded.

"That's true..."

"Are you sure you're ready for the answers?" Nick asked as Jameson's expression changed as he looked over at him and Ethan.

"You know, Alexis said the same thing when we were talking. So, you don't think I can handle this either?" Jameson asked.

"I'm not saying you can't handle it, I'm just saying be prepared and be open to anything being possible. Preparing will help it not hit as hard when you start uncovering things. That's all I mean." Nick said as Jameson nodded and agreed with him.

"I got you, I will." Jameson said.

"When did you become an expert?" Ethan asked as Nick laughed a little.

"I'm not an expert, I just know what I know. My cousin wanted to find out who her father was after her mom, who was my aunt, passed away. Well, she found him and when she went to confront him, things went left. Her mom had an affair with him and he paid her off to stay away when she told him she was pregnant, but my cousin didn't know any of that." Nick said.

"Oh wow, that's crazy. But wait, if her mom agreed to keep her a secret, how did your cousin know her father's name?" Jameson asked.

"She paid for an investigator and he gave her a name and an address so it didn't take her long to find him." Nick said.

"Why didn't the investigator tell her that he was married, so she would know how to approach going to see him?" Jameson asked as Nick shook his head.

"I don't know why he didn't tell her, but he didn't. He literally gave her a name and address without ever saying anything about him having a wife and a family of his own." Nick said.

"That's messed up. So, you said it went left, what happened?" Jameson asked.

"Well, my cousin said he came to the door and she just came out with it. She said she was his daughter and his wife overheard it, and she walked up. She asked my cousin how old she was and when she said it, the wife slapped her husband and went off. Apparently she was suspicious of him cheating at the time of conception but she never had proof. He tried denying everything but she wasn't hearing it and that was when he went off on my cousin for coming, and told her to go away. My cousin hasn't been the same since." Nick said as Jameson and Ethan glanced at each other.

"What happened to her?" Jameson asked.

"She's been in and out of mental institutions, she can't work anymore and she lives with our other aunt in Memphis." Nick said.

"I'm sorry to hear that, Nick. You think all of this triggered from that one experience?" Jameson asked.

"I'm sure there's more, but it's definitely what led her to jumping off the deep end. My cousin has two college degrees, she was making good money and doing her thing before she went looking for her dad. Now, she's living at our aunt's house on disability, taking like three different medications for mental illness. It doesn't matter now, but we feel like she would have been better off never finding out the truth. That's why I said be open to what you may find out. I think if my cousin could have been prepped a little better, things could have possibly turned out differently." Nick told him as Jameson nodded.

"I see what you're saying, and I'll definitely keep it in mind, and I will spend much time praying about it." Jameson replied as they continued looking through Damian's things.

"Bro, is this the only storage unit for Pastor Damian's stuff? I mean, so far I'm only finding a bunch of old documents from church." Ethan said.

"Yeah, I put everything in here. Keep looking, there has to be something here!" Jameson said as they continued searching.

Moments later, Jameson, Ethan and Nick were surprised when Pastor Cole Scott, III suddenly appeared at the entrance of the storage unit. He looked just as surprised as they did to see him. Pastor Scott tried to say he stopped at the wrong unit by mistake before walking away, but Jameson ran over to stop him before he walked back over to his car which was parked a couple of feet away from his truck. Jameson knew it wasn't an accident and he wanted answers.

"Pastor Scott, what are you doing here? And don't lie to me! You still have a key to my grandfather's storage unit?" Jameson asked as Nick and Ethan walked over and stood behind Pastor Scott with their arms folded.

"Hey Jameson, it's good to see you. I know it's been a while." Cole said.

"Pastor Scott, cut the small talk and answer my questions." Jameson said, sternly.

"Yes, I still have a key. I figured you would end up putting his things over here after he died and I was just checking to make sure everything was okay. I know he had a lot of valuable stuff." Cole said.

"If you're talking about his jewelry, those things are in his safe deposit box at the bank and you know that, seeing that you were his former assistant pastor." Jameson said.

"Right, I guess I forgot. I'm sorry. Here, take the key. I won't come back again." Cole said as he quickly handed Jameson his spare key to the storage unit before attempting to walk away.

"My boy is not done talking to you so, you're not going anywhere! Turn around!" Nick said as he and Ethan brushed up against him and stopped him from attempting to leave again.

"Please don't hurt me, guys, please! I know I got mad about everything and I'm sorry. Just let me leave, please." Cole pleaded.

"We're not going to hurt you, Pastor Scott. But you're not getting back into your car until you tell me why you came here, and how many visits have you made over here since my grandfather's passing?" Jameson asked.

"I only came a few times, that's it. Like I said, I was just checking on his things." Cole said.

"Why would you care about his things now, when it was you who walked away from the church, started your own and took half the members with you as payback for my grandfather not leaving the church to you in his will?" Jameson asked, sternly as Cole paused for a moment before responding.

"I know it looks bad, but I was just checking on his stuff." Cole said as Jameson gave a smirk and laughed sarcastically.

"Pastor, I'm not a violent person, but if you don't tell me the truth and stop with this lie about checking on things, I might just let my boys rough you up a bit until you start telling me what I want to know!" Jameson said, enraged as he took another step towards Cole who looked afraid.

"Just say that word, Jameson! It's whatever at this point!" Ethan replied.

"Okay, okay! I'll tell you the truth. But please, whatever you do, don't tell Dr. Carrington we had this conversation." Cole said as Jameson, Ethan and Nick looked confused.

"Did you just say Dr. Carrington? As in, my father-in-law, Dr. Carrington? How do you know Alexis' father? He never came to the church and you were never there when we did see him." Jameson said, confused by Cole's response.

"Oh my God, I can't believe this is happening right now." Cole said, shaking his head.

"You better start talking before we beat it out of you!" Nick said, sternly as Jameson attempted to calm Ethan and Nick down.

"You might as well come clean, Pastor Scott. See, I'm here today trying to find answers, answers that I believe have been kept from me all these years. Obviously there must be something here that may give me some answers for you to show up like this. Am I right?" Jameson asked as Cole sighed and nodded a little.

"Yeah, sort of..."

"Okay, start talking! I don't have all day, Pastor Scott. I have to get home soon. Why did you come here, how do you know Dr. Carrington and why are you telling me not to tell him that we spoke?" Jameson asked.

"I feel a little dizzy, can I sit down on this bench, please?" Cole asked.

"Yeah, go ahead. Nick, can you hand me that water out of the cupholder in my truck. I haven't opened it and it should still be cold." Jameson said as Nick nodded and quickly walked over to get the water out of his truck and handed it to him.

"Oh, thank you so much, Jameson. I appreciate it." Cole said, graciously as he started drinking the water.

"Why are you sweating so bad? Are you okay? Do we need to call someone?" Jameson asked, concerned.

"No, I'm okay now that I'm sitting down and I have this water. I'm just nervous. I'm okay though, thank you." Cole said.

"Alright then, I gave you what you asked for. Now answer my questions." Jameson said.

"Dr. Carrington called me and asked me to come by the storage unit to grab a file that had some items in it that he needed me to bring him." Cole said.

"Wait a minute, what? That doesn't make any sense! He asked you to come here and get a file? He barely knew my grandfather and I had no idea he knew who you were! Why would he be calling you for a file from his personal stuff? How do you two even know each other?" Jameson asked.

"Okay, I'll answer that but you said Pastor Damian and Dr. Carrington barely knew each other. You know that's not true, right?" Cole asked as

Jameson looked surprised as he glanced over at Ethan and Nick who both shook their heads.

"See what I told you bro? I told you the truth would come out, didn't I?" Ethan asked, anxiously as Jameson nodded.

"Yeah bro, you did. Pastor Scott, you're saying my grandfather and Dr. Carrington knew each other personally? You mean by way of Alexis and I being married right?" Jameson asked as Cole shook his head.

"No, they knew each other before you kids were born! The three of us go way back, Jameson. Damian didn't tell you this?" Cole asked, surprised as Jameson, Ethan and Nick glanced at each other again.

"My grandfather always said the two of you were close and had known each other for several years, it's why I was surprised when the will said that I would take over the church instead of you!" Jameson said as Cole sighed.

"So, you really didn't know the church was being left to you until the reading of the will that day?" Cole asked.

"No sir, I told you that! I had no idea! I mean, I know I was his grandson, but why choose me over someone with much more ministry experience?" Jameson asked as Cole paused for a moment before responding.

"I think I might know why." Cole said.

"Okay, can you tell me?" Jameson asked.

"Yeah, I can tell you that and more if you have some time." Cole said as Jameson, Nick and Ethan grabbed three folding chairs from inside the storage unit and sat down in front of Cole who was drinking the water Jameson gave him.

"I think I have one more water in the truck, did you need it?" Jameson asked.

"That would be great, Jameson, thank you!" Cole said as Nick rushed back over to his truck to grab it out of the other cupholder. "I don't mean to take all of your water."

"No, it's okay. You're fine." Jameson said as Nick handed the water to him before sitting next to Jameson.

"I'm just going to tell you what I know and maybe it will help you with your search. Is that okay?" Cole asked.

"Yes, that's fine!" Jameson replied, anxiously waiting to hear what Cole would tell him next.

"So I'll just start from the beginning. Damian and I are originally from Chicago, Illinois and it's where you were born before we ended up coming all the way to Florida." Cole said as Jameson reacted to what Cole told him.

"Wait, see this is already becoming too much. I was born in Chicago? My grandfather always said you grew up here and that Gainesville was where I was born! You're saying I was born in Chicago? Are you sure?" Jameson asked, surprised at what Cole was saying.

"Yes, I'm sure. I told you, Damian and I go way back and I've always been by his side so I can't make this up. You were born in the fall season, on October

9, 1991 to your mother, Shannon Montgomery." Cole said.

"My grandfather's daughter, right? Is that part still true?" Jameson asked.

"Yes, that's true. Did Damian tell you the situation surrounding your birth?" Cole asked.

"I mean, he said my mom was a teenager when she gave birth to me and that she didn't know who my biological father was, so he decided to name me after my great grandfather. Is that true?" Jameson asked as Cole paused for a moment before responding.

"Wow, is that what he said? Well, that's partially true but not all the way. Yes, it's true that your mother did get pregnant as a teenager and I'll never forget Damian's reaction. See, when Shannon found out she was pregnant, she did what any scared teenage girl would do and she told her mother first, which was your grandmother." Cole said.

"My grandfather said her name was Natalie, is that true?" Jameson asked.

"Oh yeah, that's true. I grew up with Natalie too, we all came up together. It was one Sunday after church, Natalie came in with Shannon who was in tears. Damian asked what was wrong and that was when Natalie told him that Shannon was pregnant. I was standing right there when it happened and it's a good thing I was because Damian lost it!" Cole said.

"He was upset, right?" Jameson asked.

"I mean, he was furious! But Natalie had not even told him the whole story yet, and he calmed down finally when she said there was more. Damian walked over to your mother, Shannon and grabbed her by her blouse collar like she was a dude and shook the crap out of her, asking why she was being fast and he kept asking which boy at the church got her pregnant." Cole said.

"What does *"being fast"* mean?" Jameson asked as Cole laughed a little.

"I'm sorry, I keep forgetting I'm talking to millennials. He was basically calling your mom a whore." Cole said as Jameson nodded.

"He said my mom was wild as a teenager, is that true?" Jameson asked.

"No, that's not true! That's not true at all. Damian and Natalie ran a tight ship with your mom and her sisters, they weren't allowed to do anything outside of going to church for the most part." Cole said as Jameson reacted and glanced at Ethan and Nick who were sitting next to him.

"Oh my God, so it's true! My mom wasn't an only child!" Jameson said, excitedly.

"An only child? Damian told you that too? I honestly can't say I'm surprised, but no, your mom was the oldest of six girls and the two youngest are identical twins, just like your daughters." Cole said as Jameson smiled and nodded.

"Wow, are you serious?" Jameson asked.

"Yes, it's true and I'll tell you more in a minute. Let me tell you in order so it makes sense." Cole said.

"Yes sir, that's fine. Thank you. So, you left on the day my mom tells my grandfather she's pregnant." Jameson said.

"Right! He went into a rage and I had to literally pull him off of your mom, I thought he was going to shake her to death. I sat him down in his chair so we could hear what Natalie was going to say because she kept saying there was more to what happened. Damian calmed down enough to let her explain and that's when she dropped the bombshell that Shannon was molested by the overseer of our church in Chicago at that time. His name was Apostle Shawn Anderson." Cole said as Jameson reacted to what Cole told him as he started reflecting on his conversation with Brittany from earlier that day.

"What? Your overseer molested my mom and got her pregnant? Was it just that one time?" Jameson asked, concerned.

"No, Shannon said that Shawn had been molesting her since she was 8-years-old and it continued into her teenage years. The only thing that changed was that he was paying her money under the table to keep her quiet. But that silence broke when Shannon found out she was pregnant." Cole said.

"I can't believe this, I really can't believe it. So what did my grandfather do after that? I mean, he believed her, right?" Jameson asked.

"Yeah, he believed her. But if I told you why he believed Shannon so easily, you wouldn't believe me." Cole said.

"Please tell me, Pastor Scott." Jameson said.

"I should have spoken up back then, but I didn't because part of my job was to cover my leader. Damian and Shawn were part of a large network at the time. Damian, Shawn, and several other pastors in that network would pay money to young girls between ages eighteen to twenty for sexual favors. They were supposed to always make sure the girls they chose weren't minors to keep the police or child services from ever getting involved. So, Damian knew Shawn was having sex with young girls, but he didn't know that one of those girls was his own daughter." Cole said as Jameson, Damian and Nick shook their heads in disbelief.

"So, my grandfather was cheating on my grandmother with young women in his own church? Did she know about it?" Jameson asked, disgusted.

"She didn't know about it until everything came out with Shannon getting pregnant with you. Shannon told Natalie there were other girls who were older than her that Shawn was with, she also told her mom that she saw some of those girls at their house when Natalie was out of town ministering with the women's ministry." Cole said.

"So, all you did was cover up for my grandfather and the other leaders? You weren't messing with these girls? I mean, I'm just curious." Nick said as Cole sighed and paused for a moment.

"I wasn't allowed because of my record." Cole said, shyly.

"What was on your record?" Jameson asked.

"I was a registered sex offender in Illinois for having sex with my two young daughters when they were both under the age of twelve. My wife took my daughters, divorced me and moved as far away as she could. I never saw any of them again and I had no legal right to them so I couldn't make her present them to me." Cole said as Jameson, Ethan and Nick reacted to what he said.

"Let me get this straight, you were charged, registered as a sex offender and my grandfather continued to let you be his assistant pastor knowing you would be in violation by being around young children? No one in the church had anything to say?" Jameson asked, sternly.

"No one in the church knew except for Damian. Damian had influence and he knew people in the justice system. Nothing made headlines, I did no jail time, I only had to register as a sex offender and agree to stay from all children including my own daughters. Yes, it was a violation of me still being at the church where children were, but Damian covered me as long as I didn't touch or sleep with any of them, even the ones who were of age." Cole said.

"What about your ex-wife? She didn't try to get what you did made public? I mean, she had to know how this was handled, right?" Jameson asked as Cole sighed and shook his head again.

"Just tell him!" Ethan said, sternly.

"Yeah, let's get through this so I can get you out of my face. You disgust me right now and the only reason I haven't walked away yet is because I need this information that you're giving me, and the more you talk, the more I realize that I'm not just getting answers for me, I'm getting answers that is going to help me clean up this mess my grandfather and others before me made in the lives of innocent people!" Jameson said, sternly as Cole said.

"My ex-wife, Juanita was ready to shout what happened to our daughters from the mountain tops when she saw how lenient they were being on me in the court. She tried not to do it that way to avoid the girls being exposed, but she didn't want to sit back and do nothing after hearing what the judge was letting me do. But, Damian found a way to stop her." Cole said as Jameson's expression changed.

"What do you mean he found a way to stop her? What did he do?" Jameson asked.

"I don't know who he called, but he had a couple of guys beat Juanita up. They didn't kill her, but they did enough damage to make her too afraid to say anything to anyone and they threatened to kill my daughters if they told anyone what happened. Damian knew the girls could easily identify those men and at first, he was going to go ahead have these men kill all three of them to avoid the risk of anyone talking but I begged him not to. He agreed to it with the understanding that if any of them ever got the courage to talk and expose them, I would be a dead man." Cole said.

"That doesn't make you a victim." Jameson replied.

"Yes, I know. I was just telling you how it went down." Cole said.

"So, what happened next with my mom getting pregnant. Did he protect Shawn the same way he did you?" Jameson asked.

"No, he didn't and I'll get to that part because it came later after you were born. Shannon was too far along into her pregnancy for an abortion, at least that's what Natalie said to Damian when he suggested they have the pregnancy terminated." Cole said.

"He didn't tell me that either, he didn't tell me he wanted to have me aborted." Jameson said.

"Yeah, that doesn't surprise me either. Looking back, I think Natalie just told Damian that so they wouldn't have to put Shannon through any further trauma by having one. They kept Shannon at home the entire time she was pregnant, even took her out of school and had her do her work from home. Damian's entire mindset about her pregnancy changed when they found out she was having a boy. He had six girls so this was a big deal for him." Cole said.

"So, take me to the day I was born. Grandpa said that my mom had a lot of complications and that I almost died. Is that true?" Jameson asked as Cole nodded.

"Yes, that's true, we almost lost you both when Shannon started hemorrhaging severely and the doctors were having trouble tracing you in her womb because of the amount of blood she was losing." Cole said as Jameson nodded.

"Okay, that part pretty much lines up. He said they ended up saving us both until minutes after I was born and my mom ended up dying from a heart attack." Jameson told him as Cole's expression changed.

"What? Damian said this to you?" Cole asked, surprised.

"Yes, he did. Are you telling me that's a lie too?" Jameson asked as Cole shook his head.

"Yeah Jameson, that's not true. Your mom didn't die after she gave birth to you. By the time you were born, Shannon had just turned eighteen the same day. You were born on her birthday." Cole said as Jameson reacted to what he told him.

"Are you serious? My mom and I have the same birthday?" Jameson asked.

"Yes, you do! She turned eighteen the day you were born, I can't believe Damian didn't tell you this, but with what he did, I guess I shouldn't be shocked about that either." Cole said.

"What are you talking about? What did he do?" Jameson asked.

"Damian gave Shannon less than five minutes to hold you in her arms after going through all those hours of labor and he took you away from her. He named you after your great grandfather as he said and he signed his name as the father on your birth certificate. I don't know if you ever saw that or not." Cole said.

"Yeah, I have my birth certificate. He's listed as the father but there was no one listed as the mother, not even my grandmother." Jameson said as Cole nodded.

"I didn't know that, but that doesn't surprise me either. After they left the hospital with you, I went home and I figured I would see Damian, Natalie and the girls again at church on Sunday, which was like three or four days away at the time. I called Damian a couple of times and he didn't answer, I just assumed he was busy. But he came back to church that Sunday alone." Cole said.

"He came alone?" Jameson asked, surprised.

"I'm sorry, he came to the church with you, but that was it. Natalie, Shannon and the rest of their daughters were not with him. I asked him where they were and he said that Shannon packed up her bags, got on a Greyhound bus and left town. Then he said that he and Natalie got into a fight and she packed up her things, their daughters' things and they all left. I tried to ask him what was going on and he told me to let it go. He said all I needed to know was that they were gone and that they were never coming back." Cole said as Jameson, Nick and Ethan reacted to what Cole told them.

"Did anyone ask where they were? How did he explain walking into the church with a newborn baby without anyone getting suspicious?" Jameson asked.

"I'll explain that for you too. That Sunday, Damian and I were at the church waiting for the members to arrive and that Sunday no one came. I tried calling some of the other leaders and no one was answering their phone. When we got ready to leave, Shawn Anderson and his two assistant pastors stormed into the church. Damian laid you down in the baby carrier as we both stood to face them." Cole said.

"What happened next?" Jameson asked.

"Shawn glanced over you sleeping and gave this smirk and asked if that was his son. Damian lost it and punched Shawn in the face so hard, he fell to the floor. I had to break him and one of his assistant pastors up from fighting while the other one helped Shawn get up off the floor." Cole explained.

"What happened after that?" Jameson asked.

"When they calmed down, Shawn told Damian that all of his members were at his church and were now under his ministry until further notice. They kicked Damian out of the network and shut down his ministry just like that. Shawn gave it to him so he took it away. None of the members knew about Shannon's pregnancy or about you being born. It was Shawn's baby and he wasn't about to allow himself to be exposed so he got rid of Damian and told us to never come back." Cole said.

"So is that what brought you to Florida? My grandfather wanted to start over with his ministry in a place where no one knew him?" Jameson asked.

"Yes, that's exactly it. He knew people wouldn't ask as many questions." Cole said.

"But I don't understand. It was never a secret that I was Damian's grandson, so, if you didn't know my grandfather was going with the narrative that my mother was dead, where did you think my mother was all this time?" Jameson asked.

"I asked Damian where Shannon was and he said not to ever mention Shannon because she left you and he said she wanted nothing to do with you. I didn't ask any questions after that. I don't even think any of his members asked about your mom, they just knew you were his grandson and that was it." Cole said.

"So he started his church here with you as his assistant pastor. Are you registered here in Florida as a sex offender? I'm assuming he found a way to cover you because this detail never came up before today." Jameson said.

"Yes, I'm registered and Jameson used his pull in law enforcement to keep my status from being revealed to anyone in the church. But it was on the registry and had anyone looked me up, they would have seen it. But it's a church, people didn't check things like that because they don't expect that to ever be an issue within the church." Cole said.

"This is why you worked for my grandfather all these years, he knew no job would hire a registered sex offender. Right?" Jameson asked as Cole nodded.

"Yes, that's right." Cole said.

"Wait a minute! So, is that why my grandfather left the church to me instead of you?" Jameson asked, concerned as Cole nodded again.

"It's not that Damian and I ever had a conversation about it because we didn't. But seeing as how I've been his boy and I've been there for him all these years, I just assumed I would take over if he stepped down or if anything happened to him. But when he gave it to you, I was mad, but I should not have gotten upset because deep down, I knew he was trying to protect me. He knew I would be at a greater risk of my secret getting out if I took over so he gave it to you." Cole told him.

"So, did you really take the members who left and start your own church? I mean, that's what I was told." Jameson said.

"I was going to, but I knew that would be risky so I didn't. I tried to tell the members who were following me to go back to the church and support you once I said I changed my mind about starting the church, but they felt so bad for walking away the way they did, they decided to go elsewhere. They didn't think you would receive them back so I've just been moving on with my life the best way I can." Cole said as Jameson nodded.

"I'll start by saying that if any of them desire to come back, I'll receive them and I'll understand. But that is up to them, I won't chase anyone. God has restored and I'm just doing my best to handle those who have come and entrusted me with their souls." Jameson said.

"I know you're disgusted with me and I understand. If you want me to go now I can." Cole said.

"Oh no, we're not done just yet, but we're almost there. You never told me what happened to Shawn. He kicked my dad out of his network so no one would figure out that I was his son or that he had been sleeping with his underage daughter. Is he still pastoring in Chicago? Does he have other children?" Jameson asked.

"Shawn is dead. He died when you were about a year old and yes, he had three other sons, who are your half-brothers." Cole said.

"How did he die?" Jameson asked.

"Oh God, please don't make me say it." Cole said.

"Come on, you've gone this far with me, don't hold back now. How did he die?" Jameson asked.

"Damian killed him to get revenge for what he did to Shannon and for kicking him out of his network. But he made the murder look like an accident, and even though Shawn's wife tried his hardest to fight for the police to investigate further, Shawn's death was ruled as an accident. I have no idea if Shawn's widow is still looking to get justice for him or not, I just know that his sons are now running his ministry in Chicago." Cole said.

"Did she know about me or about what he had been doing?" Jameson asked as Cole paused for a moment before responding.

"I'm not sure if she knew or not. I mean, she stayed with him but it doesn't mean she didn't know. I wouldn't be surprised if she didn't help him cover it up." Cole replied.

"What are my half-brothers' names?" Jameson asked as Cole thought for a moment.

"Fredrick, Antoine and Johnny Anderson. They're all older than you." Cole replied.

"You mean Apostle Fredrick Anderson, Sr. from Chicago?" Jameson asked.

"Yeah, you know him?" Cole asked.

"Well, I've seen him do interviews with some celebrity preachers before. I don't follow him or anything, I've just seen him around. He's my half-brother? Does he, Antoine or Johnny know about any of this?" Jameson asked.

"I seriously doubt it, or if they know, they were told a narrative that paints what they want them to see. I'm sure they see Damian as nothing more than a murderer and they probably don't know anything about you." Cole said.

"Yeah, but I did public advertising with the upgrade to the church after my grandfather died. You don't think they saw it?" Jameson asked as Cole paused for a moment before responding.

"That's possible, especially since Damian's death was the motivating factor of the instant growth with your church." Cole replied as Jameson's expression changed.

"What are you talking about? Are you saying that all the people in my ministry right now knew my grandfather from back in the day too?" Jameson asked.

"No, they didn't know him. What I mean is that God removed the shield from around the ministry that was keeping people away because God now has someone in place who was pure and who wouldn't lead people astray like your grandfather and so many others have." Cole said.

"I can see how that makes sense. But, my great grandfather was a pastor too, at least that's what my grandfather said." Jameson said.

"Yeah, I know there's a lot of things Damian said falsely or didn't tell you at all, but that part is true. Damian and I both came up under Pastor James growing up. That's why we were so close." Cole said as Jameson nodded.

"What is it?" Jameson asked.

"What?" he asked.

"I feel like you want to say something about that but you're not saying it. What is it?" Jameson asked as Cole sighed and shook his head as tears fell from his face.

"It doesn't matter, really, it doesn't matter. You're trying to find out what you need to know to help you learn more about your family, right?" Cole attempted to change the subject as more tears fell from his face.

"I have a couple of other questions that I can get to in a moment, I want to know what you're not saying about my great grandfather. It has to be deep for you to be getting emotional like this. Tell me what it is, I'm listening." Jameson said.

"I'm not saying this to blame anyone for the things I've done in my past that were wrong. I know I've done a lot of bad deeds, and I made sure I didn't do anything ever again after we got to Florida." Cole said as Jameson, Ethan and Nick glanced at each other.

"What are you talking about? What did you do?" Ethan asked.

"Yeah, because I was waiting for Jameson to ask you how many kids or young girls at our church have you touched?" Nick asked, concerned as Cole shook his head.

"I haven't touched anyone, I promise. I had a procedure done when I moved here, Damian paid for it. I basically had my genitals removed so that it would strip me of any sexual urges whatsover." Cole said as Jameson, Ethan and Nick reacted to what Cole told them.

"Are you serious? So, you could never have sex or even have the desire for sex ever again?" Nick asked, shocked.

"Yes, that's right. I know it's extreme, but it's not like I was ever going to be able to be with a woman again without my past coming up, and I didn't want to ruin any more lives like I did my own children, so I had it done." Cole said as Jameson, Nick and Ethan glanced at each other again, still in shock at what Cole told them.

"What does that have to do with my great grandfather?" Jameson asked, still confused.

"I never told you how this sick lifestyle started for me and it was what made me emotional. It started when I was a young boy at Pastor James' church." Cole said as Jameson paused for a moment before responding.

"I think I know where you're going. Are you saying that someone at my great grandfather's church molested you when you were a kid? That's how you ended up doing the things you did?" Jameson asked as Cole started to cry more and he nodded his head as Ethan handed him some tissue.

"Yes, that's right. Like I said, I know I can't blame people for what I did to my daughters, but I didn't wake up wanting to hurt young girls. I had dreams of one day preaching and becoming a pastor like you that made a difference in people's lives. I even had a desire to become a doctor one day too, but all of that changed for me when I was 9-years-old." Cole said.

"That's when you got molested?" Jameson asked.

"Yes, that's when it started and it didn't end until right after I turned eighteen and got ready to graduate from high school." Cole said as Jameson, Nick and Ehtan shook their heads.

"I'm sorry to hear that, Pastor Scott, we all are." Jameson said as Nick and Ethan agreed with him.

"Thank you. I never told anyone except one person, and I never got help or any of that until after I did the things I did to my daughters. Had I known being molested would take me down the path it did, I would have gotten help sooner, I just didn't know how to ask for it. I was too busy covering for everyone else." Cole said.

"You said you told one person, was it my grandfather?" Jameson asked.

"Yes, I told Damian right after we graduated from high school. He felt bad and it's why he helped me out the way he did all these years, even after he died." Cole said as Jameson's expression changed.

"What do you mean after he died?" Jameson asked.

"His life insurance policy, I was the beneficiary for two million dollars and that's what I've been living off of." Cole said.

"Hold on, I'm confused. I was listed as the beneficiary on his policy. Why do you think I've been able to do so much upgrading with the church? I mean, I make good money in my career, but I've used a lot of the money he left me to upgrade things in the ministry. The will never said anything about him having a second beneficiary." Jameson said, confused as Cole nodded.

"I told you, your grandfather had his way of covering his bases. Damian had another policy that he took out on himself and it was private. Dwayne didn't even know about it. It was a two million dollar policy with me as the sole beneficiary and you were listed secondary in case something happened to me before he died. He did that because I had moments where I was suicidal so he just wanted to make sure." Cole said.

"Wow, I did not know that." Jameson said.

"Yeah, his lawyer knew but he was not to reveal that information to anyone except for me." Cole said.

"He did all of this because he felt sorry for you being molested when you were growing up in my great grandfather's church?" Jameson asked, surprised.

"Well yeah, but there's some more to it than that." Cole said.

"What do you mean?" Jameson asked.

"See, I never told you who it was who molested me, but I told Damian. When I told him, that was what made him feel guilty because he didn't know." Cole said.

"I'm sorry, I'm still confused. So, who molested you?" Jameson asked.

"Your great grandfather did it, Pastor James molested me all those years." Cole said as Jameson, Nick and Ethan reacted to what he said. "I promise you I'm not lying."

"No, I don't think that, I'm just shocked because I never knew that about my great grandfather. My grandfather always spoke well about him. Why would he feel that he should have protected you when you were both young children at the time? I mean, if anyone should have protected you, it should have been your own parents!" Jameson said, defensively.

"Yeah, you're right. But my father wasn't around and my mom only cared about sleeping with random men for money. She didn't have time for me or my sister who ended up killing herself when she was fifteen after being brutally raped some guy our mom had let in the house. My mom didn't believe her and she couldn't take it. It was crazy because suicides back then were almost unheard of. So I had no one looking out for me like that, that's what Pastor James said he would do for me and for a while he did, but then he took advantage of me." Cole said.

"Pastor Scott, I am so sorry. I am so sorry to hear that. So was my grandfather carrying the guilt of not knowing it was happening to you until years later? Jameson asked.

"That was only part of it. Damian thought that as long as he allowed it to happen to him, Pastor James wouldn't go after any other boys." Cole said as Jameson reacted to what Cole said to him.

"What? Pastor, are you saying that my great grandfather molested his own son? He molested my grandfather when he was a kid too?" Jameson asked, disgusted.

"Yes, he did and he did to Damian's brother, Ricky too. I don't know if he told you about your great uncle or not." Cole said.

"Yes, Derrick Elgin Montgomery, right?" Jameson asked.

"Yeah, that's him. Ricky went to prison carrying that pain and I found out last year when I looked him up that he had hung himself in prison years ago. Somehow, Damian never knew about it. I guess he wasn't listed as next of kin so he wasn't notified." Cole said.

"Okay, I get why he took care of you all these years, but I don't understand why my grandfather named me after the man who stole your innocence. My grandfather had all these good things to say about my great grandfather!" Jameson said, confused after everything Cole told him.

"I think Damian knew telling the truth on that end would mean he would have to face his own pain and he didn't want to do that. He wanted to remember his dad before the molestation, and I think he named you after him so that you could do the things that Pastor James should have done when it comes to the church and the people. A lot of people have been hurt and damaged and it started with Pastor James and it just trickled down. There's still so much I haven't told you, Jameson. Just hear me when I tell you that leader wounds are the worst! Leader wounds are what caused everything I've told you so far." Cole said.

"Wait a minute, I remember hearing my grandfather say that to me before he died. It was during the last conversation we had. He said leader wounds are the most dangerous and I asked him if his wounds had been healed, and he said yes. But he wouldn't tell me much about it, only very little and the little he did say wasn't fully the truth. He's done so much damage, but damage was done to him first." Jameson said as tears fell from his face while Nick and Ethan did their best to comfort him.

"I probably should get going." Cole said as he got ready to stand up.

"Wait a minute, wait! So, my mom and grandmother are still alive! Right?" Jameson asked.

"As far as I know they are, but I don't know for sure, Jameson. All I know is that the story Damian told about your mom dying giving birth to you isn't true. He took you to raise himself and sent Shannon away because he always wanted sons, he never wanted daughters. That's probably why he said Shannon was his only child because had it not been for the fact that he had you, he would pretend like he didn't have six daughters altogether. So there is a chance that your mother is still alive and you can get an investigator to help you locate her if you want." Cole said.

"Or I could use social media right?" Jameson asked.

"Based on what I believe happened with Natalie and your mom's other sisters after you were born, I doubt if any of them have social media of any kind. You can try a google search, but they may have changed their names to ensure that Damian never found them. He was dangerous and I truly believe that your grandmother took her daughters, who are your aunts and she ran away in fear of her life and theirs." Cole said.

"Is it because my grandfather killed Shawn? Is that what scared her?" Jameson asked.

"Damian didn't go after Shawn until a year after you were born. Natalie, Shannon and the rest of her sisters were long gone before then. I know why he sent Shannon away, but Natalie took their daughters out of fear for her life." Cole replied.

"So, you think he threatened them or something?" Jameson asked, concerned.

"I know he did. I didn't witness it, but I know he did it. If you remember, I told you that their two youngest daughters are identical twins. Well, when Natalie got pregnant with them, the doctor made a mistake and told them they were having twin boys." Cole said as Jameson, Nick and Ethan glanced at each other.

"Are you serious?" Jameson asked.

"Yeah, the doctor messed up big time. She told them they were having twin boys the entire pregnancy and Damian was so excited. They really weren't planning to have anymore kids, but Damian got over it when found out he was having two sons because he had been wanting boys for a long time. But the day that Natalie went into labor and the babies were born, the truth came out. They didn't have twin boys, they had identical twin girls." Cole said.

"That is crazy! How do you make a mistake like that and not realize it until the babies are born?" Jameson asked, surprised.

"I don't know but she made the mistake, and she was a seasoned doctor! The same doctor who had delivered their other four children. Damian blamed Natalie after that. He would vent to me at times saying how it was Natalie's fault for not paying more attention that she got pregnant again. Really, he was angry that he now had six daughters that he didn't want and finding out that his two youngest were girls instead of boys the way he did really set him off and I think he threatened to hurt them and Natalie finally decided to get away." Cole said.

"So you don't think he killed her or them?" Jameson asked as Cole shook his head.

"No, he didn't kill them. But he was probably going to and that's why she ran. I have no idea where they are and I can't promise that they are alive, but there is still a chance. Just be prepared for the outcome when you do start searching. Can I go now? I didn't mean to be here this long." Cole said.

"Wait, that's what we never talked about. You came here because Dr. Carrington sent you and you said that he knew my grandfather from Chicago. Alexis just told me that both of her parents grew up there and it made me wonder." Jameson said.

"Oh yeah, I forgot. So wait, did Bobby marry Crystal?" Cole asked as Jameson nodded.

"Yes, his wife's name is Crystal!" Jameson said, anxiously as Cole nodded.

"Is your wife their oldest?" Cole asked as Jameson nodded.

"Yeah, she's the oldest and she's a year older than me." Jameson told him.

"Okay, so they had a daughter. Bobby and Crystal were about a year or two older than your mother, and they were training in Damian's church to become ministers." Cole said as Damian, Nick and Ethan reacted to what he said.

"Are you serious? I don't even think they told Alexis that! They were training to become ministers at my grandfather's church?" Jameson asked.

"What happened?" Nick asked.

"Yeah, they were until Damian kicked them out of the church after Crystal found out she was pregnant with Alexis. You know fornication is a sin and it was frowned upon in the church network. Damian would have had to face the board of panelists in Shawn's organization if he found out two of his ministers in training had sex and got pregnant. He didn't want that, so he kicked them out and when Shawn asked about them, he said that Bobby and Crystal decided to leave the ministry to relocate and focus on school. Shawn was a little suspicious but he let it go and that was it. I never saw Bobby or Crystal again until we got to Gainesville and Damian called me the day he went to your school and saw them. Alexis was in your class, right?" Cole asked.

"Yes, she was. That's how we met. Are you serious? So, that's why they wanted nothing to do with the church and that's why they don't come now." Jameson said.

"Right. I'm kind of surprised they allowed you and Alexis to get as close as you guys did knowing who you were related to. I guess they decided not to let their personal grudge get in the way of your relationship." Cole said.

"Okay, so I got it. But why did he send you to my grandfather's storage unit? What did he want you to get?" Jameson asked.

"There's a file in Damian's stuff that has the proof that would help the police solve Shawn Anderson's murder." Cole said as Jameson looked surprised.

"Are you serious? Okay, why does he want it now? I mean, my grandfather is gone so it's not like he could be arrested for it." Jameson said, confused on why Bobby wanted this information for himself.

"I learned to stop asking questions, but he asked for it so I was going to give it to him. I'm just going to change my number, pack my stuff and get out of here before he comes tracking me down when I don't bring him what he asked for. I need to go. Listen, you will find what I came for in a box that says "forbidden files." You will also find a photo of your grandmother, your mom, and her five sisters. If you turn the photo over, it has each of their names on the back and their birthdates. But remember, they may have changed their names by now and that's assuming all of them are still alive. I hope they are. With Damian being gone, people don't need to live in fear anymore. I have to go." Cole said.

"Wait, Pastor Scott, take my card. You can call me anytime and thank you so much for taking time to tell me all of this. I'll be praying for you and if you need me, I'm here. I mean it." Jameson said as he and Cole hugged each other and tears fell from Cole's face again.

"Thank you, Jameson, I appreciate it and I'm sorry for how I handled things. I hope you can forgive me." Cole said.

"You were forgiven a long time ago, we're good. Take care of yourself." Jameson replied as Cole shook Nick and Ethan's hand before rushing to get in his car and drive away.

It was getting late in the afternoon by the time Jameson finished his conversation with Cole, and he saw that Alexis was texting him to see what time he would be home for dinner. Jameson replied to her message and said he would be there in an hour before rushing back into the storage unit with Nick and Ethan to retrieve the information that Cole told them about. As they looked through the box, they weren't able to find the file that Cole said Bobby sent him to the storage unit to retrieve. They checked a couple of other boxes thinking that it was possibly moved someplace else, but they still didn't find anything. Jameson knew he didn't have much time left and he decided to check back for it later on and kept his focus finding the picture that would have his grandmother, his mom and her sisters on it. Jameson found the photo and tears fell from his face as he looked at them and saw their names on the back. Jameson's mother was beautiful and his daughters resembled her in a lot of ways. Jameson put the photo back into the box and decided to take the entire box home so that he could spend more time later on looking through the rest of it.

Jameson, Ethan and Nick left the storage unit and quickly locked it back up before driving away as it started to get dark outside. When Jameson arrived home, carrying the box inside the house with him,

Alexis was setting up the table for dinner and feeding their children who were sitting at the table. Jameson quickly put the box down when they ran over to greet him after not seeing him all day long. Jameson then hugged and kissed Alexis, and explained what the box was as they walked over to the table. After the day he had with Cole, he wanted to unwind and process everything he learned before telling Alexis about it. So, he took advantage of their family time during dinner in a way he never had before, because today made him appreciate his family and the call of God on his life in a deeper way. Jameson was initially planning to tell Alexis everything that happened today after the kids were put to bed, but after the kids were asleep, Jameson heard God speak to him, and God told him not to tell Alexis about any of it until he released him to do it. Jameson never kept things from his wife and he didn't know why God was wanting him to wait, but he decided to obey what he heard God say and not tell his wife about today's events. He then sent a text message to Ethan and Nick letting them know his plans so they wouldn't mention any of it around her, or even Dwayne.

Nearly a month had gone by and the Lord still had not released Jameson to tell his wife anything, and the suspense was killing him. Jameson was saddened to learn that Cole had passed away after committing suicide inside of a Las Vegas hotel room. Even though Jameson offered to be there for Cole, he also knew that Cole was in a state of pain and was in need of more help than he could possibly provide to him, but he still desired to help him and even offered to get services for him where he stayed, but Cole never got back to him. Jameson felt guilty at first, but Nick and Ethan encouraged him not to blame himself for a choice that Cole made on his own. Jameson learned that the sooner someone can get help, the better. He also learned that it's never too late to get help and when a person has the right support, they won't feel the need to live their lives suffering in silence.

Over the last two weeks, Jameson made additional changes to the ministry by hiring Christian trauma counselors to come and provide counseling to any members in his church that were dealing had dealt with sexual trauma or other emotional traumas that they had not yet dealt with. To ensure that no one felt embarrassed about getting the help they needed, Jameson's new secretary that he hired set up an online scheduling system on the church's website that allowed the members and the leaders to schedule sessions with one of the counselors privately without anyone having to know what they were doing, and the system worked perfectly. Several of Jameson's members and leaders signed up and started receiving help from the counselors. While Jameson had been gearing his teachings towards healing from past hurt and having mass deliverance services that allowed people to receive prayer, he wanted to make sure that counseling resources were available as well so that no one would have to function in ministry another day with open wounds that had not yet been healed.

Other local pastors in the community asked for Jameson's help with getting those same services in their church so that they could better help and support members within their ministry who had experienced past trauma. Jameson's efforts started to attract media attention, which led to him having interviews where he provided the steps he had taken with his ministry on national live television. Emails and letters were flooding in from pastors around the world who were offering to pay Jameson good money for the opportunity to help them get resources for their members, and knowing how to talk to members of their ministry who are dealing with trauma. Jameson limited his assistance to paid virtual gatherings with leaders where he provided the information to them so that he wouldn't be away from his family, so that he could focus on getting the closure he desired to have by doing whatever it took to locate his grandmother, mother and her five sisters. Jameson's plans to hire a private investigator were also changed when the Lord told him to wait before moving forward with that decision. Jameson didn't understand why God was having him approach things this way, but he trusted God enough to wait for his directions and not do anything on his own.

It was another Friday morning and Jameson was excited for the opportunity to talk to a group of students at the University of Florida campus after his youth pastor, Quincy Washington connected the leader of their organization at an event and came up with the idea to have Jameson speak and share resources and information that would help their students feel confident to get the help they need without living in fear of being judged or questioning their faith in God.

Jameson prepared for this gathering not knowing that after today, he would begin to see why the Lord had him wait on telling his wife about his conversation with Pastor Scott and hiring a private investigator to help him locate his mom and her side of the family. Alexis has been in Ft. Lauderdale this week for a business conference and was planning to return home by Monday. Jameson dropped his kids off at their grandparents' house before being picked up by Nick and Ethan to head to the campus for today's event. When they arrived, Quincy was standing outside with the campus ministry organization leader, Carlos Joseph, who is a junior at the university. After spending a few minutes talking and introducing themselves to one another, Quincy and Carlos led Jameson, Nick and Ethan to the conference room where the event was held. When they walked inside, Jameson was surprised by the number of students that were inside waiting because he was expecting it to be a much smaller group. Jameson spoke and opened the floor for questions at the end, which unexpectedly opened up the opportunity for Jameson to minister several of the students that asked their questions. Before the meeting ended, Jameson asked Carlos if it was okay for him to pray for different people and Carlos allowed him to do it.

Several people came to the altar for prayer, Nick and Ethan assisted Jameson as he began to pray for each person, and Jameson was in shock at how God was using him at this meeting. It wasn't because God had never used him to minister to people or pray for them, but this moment was the first time that Jameson began to prophesy to the people that the Lord was allowing him to pray for. Jameson had never prophesied to anyone before, he was never told he was called to that office because growing up, his grandfather did not allow prophecy within their church, and even though he made changes after Damian passed away, Jameson continued to hold to not allowing anyone to prophesy in his church. But in this very moment, Jameson's mind shifted and he didn't hold back on how God was using him even though it was something new that he had never experienced or walked in before. When the meeting was over, Nick and Ethan were still in shock about what happened and they kept asking Jameson when he learned how to prophesy like that. Jameson didn't know how to answer them, he said that it felt like he had been doing it for a long time even though today was his first time. Nick and Ethan were supportive even though they didn't know much about it either, and they were open to being taught more about it in the near future. Nick and Ethan's response made Jameson feel good and gave him the courage to find a way to teach on the prophetic at his own church when the time was right and once he had time to study it more in depth for himself.

After spending time shaking hands and talking to different students for an hour or so after the gathering was over, Jameson finally got ready to leave

with Ethan and Nick. As Carlos and Quincy walked
with them to the parking deck where their car was,
they heard a voice from afar yelling for Jameson to
stop. When they stopped and turned around, they
saw three young men who appeared to be students
running towards them from the opposite end of the
hallway they were in.

"Do you guys know them?" Jameson asked,
curiously as they watched them run in their
direction.
"Oh wow, yes! Yes, we know them! As a matter
of fact, they're last name is Montgomery too!" Carlos
said.
"It is?" Jameson asked.
"Yeah, Jamaal is a graduate student and he's
student government president so he's popular. The
other two are his younger brothers, Javon and Jarrell.
Javon is on the basketball team and Jarrell is on the
football team." Carlos added as Jameson, Ethan and
Nick reacted to what he told them.
"Oh my God, I thought they were familiar!
We've seen them play before, that's Javon and Jarrell
Montgomery?" Ethan asked.
"Yeah, that's them! Hey guys!" Carlos said as
Jamaal, Javon and Jarrell stopped where they were
and greeted them.
"What's good, Carlos! I'm sorry we missed the
gathering today, we were tied up with some stuff. But
we saw the recording from the area we were in."
Jamaal said.

"You guys recorded this?" Jameson asked, surprised.

"Oh yeah, we forgot to tell you it was being recorded. The whole campus saw it! Right, Carlos?" Quincy asked as Jameson, Ethan and Nick became excited.

"Yeah, that's right. We could only have a certain number of people in the conference room we were in and I hated that we couldn't get a bigger space because of some other events that were happening today. So we found a way to have the media team live stream it from the campus ministry's site, Facebook, and Instagram. They were in the booth in the back so you may not have seen them, but everyone saw you! You rocked it today, Jameson! I didn't know you were a prophet!" Quincy said.

"Neither did I!" Jameson said as everyone started laughing. "Guys, I don't mean to be rude. How are you doing? I'm Jameson Montgomery, I'm the senior pastor here in Gainesville at Back To Life Church." Jameson said as he shook Jamaal, Jarrell and Javon's hand.

"Wow, it's nice to meet you! Yeah, we were watching from the game center on the other side of the campus and your testimony was awesome! We left as soon as you were done sharing it so we could catch you before you left, because you helped us!" Jamaal said.

"Can you guys sign our planner? We love watching you play!" Nick said as Jameson started laughing.

"Sure, no problem! Thanks for the support!" Jarrell said as he and Javon signed their planner as they asked.

"Listen, I know you're getting ready to leave but we really need to talk to you. There's a reason why we ran all the way from the other side of campus to talk to you." Jamaal said as Jameson looked over at Carlos and Quincy.
"I mean, that's fine with us. We're pretty much done here, we were just going to walk you to the garage before I head to my next class." Carlos said.
"Well, we don't want to make you late. We can talk to them and I'll walk them to the parking deck if that's okay." Quincy said.
"Sure, that's fine! Guys, it was so great meeting you and Pastor Jameson, thank you again for coming to talk to our students. They're never going to forget this and we have to bring you back soon!" Carlos said as he and Jameson hugged each other.
"You're welcome, Carlos. I have your number so I'll be in touch and you reach out to me anytime you need to." Jameson said.
"Thank you so much, I will." Carlos said as he shook Ethan and Nick's hand. "I have to get going but you guys have a great day! Jamaal, I'll see you, Javon and Jarrell tomorrow right?" Carlos asked as they shook hands.
"Yeah, we'll be there by nine. I'll call you." Jamaal said as Carlos nodded before walking away.
"Okay, where can we sit and talk?" Jameson asked as he started to look around.

"We can go right over here." Javon said as he led them to a pavilion that was just outside of the building they were in.

"Thank you again for taking time to talk to us at the last minute." Jarell said.

"It's my pleasure." Jameson said.

"Do you need us to give you some privacy while you guys talk?" Ethan asked.

"Oh no, it's okay. You can stay." Javon said.

"Okay, great! I'm all ears." Jameson said, anxiously waiting to hear what they have to say.

"I'm going to start by showing you something, first." Jamaal said as he pulled out his cell phone and went to take a picture on his phone. "Pastor, do you know the woman in this picture with us?"

"Can I look at that for a moment?" Jameson asked as Jamaal nodded and handed him his phone.

"That's us and our mom. Her name is Shannon Montgomery." Jamaal said as Jameson, Ethan and Nick reacted to what he said.

"Oh my God! Your mom's name is Shannon Montgomery? How recent is this picture?" Jameson asked.

"We took it with her last week." Jamaal said as tears fell from Jameson's face.

"Oh my God, I can't believe it. I can't believe it!" Jameson said in shock.

"So, do you know her? We're asking because after we heard you share your testimony, we started thinking about the things our mom has been telling us over the years. She told us she had another son and that we had an older brother, but she never told his name. But when we heard you share and we realized you shared our last name, we couldn't help but wonder if you were our brother." Jamaal said as he, Javon and Jarrell tried to maintain their composure.

"Oh my God, I can't believe it. I never met my biological mother before, but I know that her name is Shannon Michele Montgomery and she gave birth to me in Chicago, Illinois on her eighteenth birthday, October 9, 1991. Is her middle name Michele?" Jameson said as Jamaal, Javon and Jarrell started crying.
"Oh my God, Jameson, you're our brother! You're our brother!" Jamaal said, excitedly as he started to break down.
"Our mom's middle name is Michele and she told us that she was originally from Chicago, and that she gave birth to you on her eighteenth birthday. We've heard the story a million times growing up, but she's never been able to tell us much more than that without crying. We've been trying for years to get her to tell us more about her upbringing." Javon said.
"Yeah, and every time we asked her what happened to her baby, she kept saying he was taken away but she never said anything else." Jarrell added.

"Our mother battles with severe mental illness. She has Post Traumatic Stress Disorder (PTSD), Manic Depression, Anxiety Disorder, Bipolar Disorder, Schizophrenia and Multiple Personality

Disorder. She does okay when she's on her meds, but she's been in and out of mental institutions for as long as we can remember. She's in a facility right now. We took that picture last week when we went to visit her and we tried not to trigger her by pressuring her to tell us more information, but we've wanted to find our brother for years!" Jamaal said.

"We knew if we found you, we could probably get the answers to questions we've wanted the answers to for years!" Jamaal said as Jameson nodded while continuing to look at the photo.

"Who's the other guy in this picture with you? Is that our brother too?" Jameson asked.

"Yeah, that's Jacoby! He's the oldest! Well, sort of. He was the oldest in the house since we didn't know who you were." Javon said as Jameson said.

"So, that's why Mom made sure our names started with the letter "J," she wanted to remember Jameson. I just don't know why she never told us your name." Jarrell said.

"I know why, and we can talk about that." Jameson said.

"So, you believe us, Pastor Jameson? You believe we're your brothers? I know we don't have birth certificates or anything to show you." Jamaal said.

"You can call me Jameson and yes, I believe you're my brothers. I finally had the chance to see a picture of our mother when she was a young girl last week when I went looking through our grandfather's old things and this picture looks just like her. So, I believe it! I just had no idea that she had other children or that she was even alive all this time." Jameson said as Jamaal, Javon, and Jarrell glanced at each other.

"What do you mean? You thought she died?" Javon asked.

"Yeah, that's what I was told. I was told she died after giving birth to me, but I only learned recently that it wasn't true and that there was still a chance she was still alive. I've been looking ever since, and I was actually going to hire a private investigator to find out where she was, but God told me to wait. He told me to wait and now I see why. God knew that he was going to send you to me! I've never had siblings and I'm honored to know that I have four younger brothers who are doing such great things! It's so nice to finally meet all of you!" Jameson said, excitedly as they got up from the table and began to hug and embrace each other as Nick, Ethan and Quincy stood nearby smiling and watching them as they had their moment. They knew how long Jameson had been waiting for this to happen.

"Wow, I have so much to tell you and there's so much for us to talk about. I don't even know if there's enough time. I don't want to hold up my leaders from getting back home and I definitely don't want to keep you guys from getting to where you need to go." Jameson said.

"We have all the time you need! Our classes are done for the day!" Jamaal said.

"Yeah, and we don't have practice again until tomorrow since there's no game tonight. We can keep talking if you have time." Jarrell said.

"Did you drive to campus?" Jamaal asked.

"Quincy did, but I came with Nick and Ethan in Nick's truck." Jameson said.

"Okay, cool. If you guys want to leave, I can bring Jameson home when we're done." Jamaal said.

"Yeah, that works. Are you good with that Jameson?" Ethan asked.

"Yeah, that's fine. Thank you guys so much for staying, I appreciate it. Nick, can you and Ethan go by Crystal's house and check on my kids? Tell her what I'm doing and that I'll come by later on. If she needs to leave to do anything without the kids around, can you take them with you until I get home?" Jameson asked.

"We got you covered, Jameson, don't worry. We will keep you posted on everything once we get over there." Nick said as he slapped hands with Jameson.

"Thank you guys, so much! I appreciate it. I'll call you when I get back a little later." Jameson told them as Nick, Ethan and Quincy said goodbye to all of them before walking away.

"Wow, you have kids?" Jamaal asked.

"Yes, I do! I have my son, Jameson, Jr. but we call him by his middle name, Isaiah. He's five and these are my 2-year-old twin girls, Destiny and Victoria." Jameson replied, showing them pictures on his phone.

"So, this is our nephew and our two nieces?" Jarrell asked.

"That's right! They're going to love you when you meet them." Jameson said.

"They are beautiful! So you're married?" Javon asked.

"Yes, this is my wife, Alexis. She's out of town on business, but she'll be back on Monday." Jameson said, showing them more pictures.

"Dang, that's your wife? She is fine!" Javon said as Jamaal nudged him and everyone started laughing.

"Excuse him, please!" Jamaal said.

"My bad bro!" Javon said.

"You're okay, I get that reaction a lot. My wife is beautiful." Jameson told them.

"So, how long have you been in Gainesville? I mean, it must be a long time for you to have an entire church here?" Jamaal asked.

"Yeah, I've been in Gainesville since I was about a year old and I'm thirty-one now. How old are you guys? I'm just curious seeing how you're all in college." Jameson asked.

"Well, Jacoby is twenty-five, I'm a year younger than Jacoby, Javon is twenty-two and Jarrell is twenty." Jamaal said as Jameson nodded.

"So, Mom waited a while before she had more children. Do you have the same father?" Jameson asked as the guys shook their heads.

"Jacoby and I have the same father, Javon and Jarrell both have different fathers. Our dad died when

Mom was pregnant with me. Javon's dad is serving life in prison for murder and Jarrell's dad lives in New York, and he's currently paying $1,500.00 a month in back child support to Jarrell every month." Jamaal said.

"Wow, Mom took his dad to court?" Jameson asked.

"No, Jacoby did it when he realized Jarrell's father was still alive and living in New York where he's an accountant who makes plenty of money. He paid for the attorney and everything. He hated that he couldn't do much to get any back payments from Javon's father with him being in prison, but he's still looking to see what can be done." Jamaal said as Jameson nodded.

"So, Jacoby has really looked out for you guys, huh?" Jameson asked.

"Yeah, he was like our big brother and our father. He made sure we did well in school and he really took care of us when our mom couldn't. We all decided to stay here for college so that our mom wouldn't feel alone. We didn't know how she would take us away so we stayed." Javon said.

"I understand and I commend all of you. How does Mom feel about what you've accomplished and what you're doing now?" Jameson asked.

"She supports us! She's proud of us for achieving goals with school and other things because she wasn't able to do it." Jarrell said as Jameson nodded.

"Who did you grow up with, Jameson? Did you know your dad?" Jamaal asked as Jameson took a deep breath before responding.

"No, my biological father was killed when I was almost a year old and we never met. My story is long, twisted and complicated. But I want to try and explain it all to you, and I would even like to meet our mom when the time is right. I mean, do you think she's ready to see me?" Jameson asked as Jamaal, Javon and Jarrell glanced at each other.

"It's hard to say. But, when you meet Jacoby, we'll see what he says about the right time for Mom to see you." Javon said.

"Not a problem, just let me know. I actually grew up with our grandfather, who was our mom's dad." Jameson said as they reacted to what he told them.

"Are you serious? You know our grandfather?" Jarrell asked.

"Yeah, I knew him. He raised me as his own son and he was the pastor of the church before he died and left the church to me." Jameson said.

"Wow! He was a pastor too? Mom never let us go to church, ever! We never heard anything about God or the Bible until we got to college and met Carlos. He talks to us sometimes and we're not a Christian like you guys, but we still listen to him. It's just a lot to take in because we never heard it before." Jamaal said as Jameson nodded.

"I understand and don't think that because I'm a pastor, I'm going to force you into anything you're not ready for. Once I tell you everything, you're going to understand why Mom kept you from the church and never taught you anything about God." Jameson said as they nodded.

Jameson spent the rest of the afternoon talking and catching up with Jamaal, Javon and Jarrell. He told them everything he knew after his recent conversation with Cole, and Jamaal, Javon and Jarrell shared things with him as well that helped him connect the dots even more. Jameson wasn't surprised when he realized that Jamaal, Javon and Jarrell weren't aware that their mom had five younger sisters who she had not seen since she was 18-years-old, along with their her mother, who is their grandmother. By the end of their conversation, Jameson didn't feel that he was any closer to finding out where his grandmother, Natalie and his five aunts were located because they didn't know. Jameson's prayer was that when he finally had the chance to see and meet his biological mother for the first time, that she would feel comfortable to open up and talk about her life in a way she never has with anyone before because she would be assured that this time around, she was safe and she did not have to worry about anyone ever hurting her or keeping her in a place of captivity again.

When Jameson got ready to leave with his brothers, he received a text message from his mother-in-law, Crystal who said she was aware of what he was doing and agreed to keep his children overnight so he wouldn't have to rush home. Jameson replied and thanked her for doing it and he was very appreciative to her for her support. She then sent another message that said that if he had time tomorrow, he wanted the two of them to talk about some things when he came over to pick his children up from their house.

Jameson replied and said they would talk and he immediately began to wonder if she was going to open up and tell them the truth that he newly learned from his conversation with Cole. If so, he couldn't help but wonder what would happen if Bobby overheard their conversation and he knew it would be important that they didn't speak too loud about it since Bobby was not aware of how much Jameson knew. Fifteen minutes later, Jameson arrived at Jacoby's house with Jamaal, Javon and Jarrell who decided to surprise him with the news when they called him to make sure he was home before coming over. Jamaal lived in a very nice house not far from the campus and he welcomed Jameson into his home with open arms not knowing he was talking to his long lost brother.

"It's nice to meet you, Jameson! Can I get you anything to eat or drink?" Jacoby asked as they sat at the dining room table near the kitchen.

"I'll take some water, thank you." Jameson said as Jacoby nodded and quickly went to grab a bottle of Fiji water out of the fridge and hand it to him as he joined the rest of them at the table.

"Alright, guys what's going on? You brought Jameson here and said you had some kind of surprise for me or something. What's the surprise?" Jacoby asked as he took another sip of his wine and closed his laptop as Jamaal, Javon and Jarrell smiled and glanced at each other.

"I did all the talking at school, your turn to talk Javon!" Jamaal said as Javon nudged him.

"Okay fine, I'll talk this time. Jacoby, I know this will shock you but we met Jameson today for the first time when he came to speak at our campus. He shared his testimony and after spending the last few hours talking to him, we made a new discovery." Javon said as Jacoby glanced at Jameson looking confused.

"A new discovery? What are you talking about, Javon?" Jacoby asked.

"Jacoby, this is him! This is our big brother that Mom has been talking about all these years. This is Jameson Isaiah Montgomery, Sr. He's our brother!" Javon said, excitedly as Jacoby immediately looked over at Jameson and tears welled up in his eyes and slowly fell from his face.

"Guys, don't play with me! Are you serious? This is really him?" he asked, trying not to break down.

"Yes bro, we wouldn't make this up. Jameson is our brother, this is him!" Jarrell said as Jacoby quickly got up from the table and walked over to Jameson who stood up and hugged him as he broke down crying.

"Oh my God, I can't believe it! It's really you! It's really you! I've been praying for this moment my whole life!" Jacoby said as he and Jameson continued to hug and embrace each other as Jameson started crying again.

"Yes Jacoby, it's me. I'm here!" Jameson replied as they both sat next to each other at the table as Javon and Jarrell moved to the other end of the table.

"I can't believe I'm crying like this." Jacoby said as they started laughing and Jamaal handed them both some tissue.

"It's okay, Jacoby, we've been crying for hours!" Jameson said as they laughed again.

"I thought you looked familiar, but I had no idea. So, Shannon is your mother?" Jacoby asked, still in shock as Jameson nodded.

"Yes, she is!" he said.

"So, you were born on October 9th?" Jacoby asked.

"Yes, that's right. Just like her, I was born on her eighteenth birthday." Jameson said as Jacoby nodded.

"I can't believe it's really you! We've been in the same city and didn't even know it!" Jacoby said.

"Yes, I know! That's what we were talking about today." Jameson said as he, Jamaal, Jarrell and Javon began to explain everything leading up to this moment to Jacoby.

"So you're not sure if our grandmother is still alive?" Jacoby asked.

"No, I'm not sure but I'm hoping to find that out soon." Jameson said.

"Mom has five younger sisters? Are you sure? I mean, I know she never told us your name but she

always said she had another son that she gave birth
to on her birthday. She never said anything about her
mom, dad or having five sisters. Why would she leave
that out?" Jacoby asked, confused.

"I'm not sure, but she does. I have the picture
and information at home to prove it. She has five
younger sisters named Tracey, Bridgette, Monica,
and identical twins, Lauren and Lindsey. But Mom
hasn't seen them since she gave birth to me."
Jameson said.
"Wow, this is so crazy. I mean, I want to know
where they are too and why they never came looking
for their sister? Why didn't our grandmother come
looking for her daughter?" Jacoby asked, concerned.
"I'm not sure, but there's so many twists and
turns to everything. There's still a lot more for me to
share with all of you and I will, but I need you to do
your best to keep an open mind and not to judge any
of them because they've been through a lot." Jameson
said as Jacoby and the rest of his brothers nodded.
"So, you're ready to meet our mom?" Jacoby
asked.
"I've been ready! But, the guys told me about
her mental illness and I am more than happy to meet
our mom when she's ready. I mean, has she ever said
anything about meeting me or wanting to see me?"
Jameson asked.
"She always said she missed you and that she
wished she could hold you again. I mean, that's a
pretty good sign that she wants to see you. But I do
want to make sure she's ready by seeing how she

responds when we tell her that we found each other."
Jacoby said as Jameson nodded.

"Jameson, can you bring anything with you
that you think could help refresh her memory even
more? Or at least assure her that we're not lying to
her, because she's going to be blown away." Javon
said.
"Yes, I can bring the information I told you
guys about. Just tell me when and where to meet you,
and I'll come. How much longer is she going to be at
this facility?" Jameson asked.
"I think they're releasing her next Friday as
long as she remains stable as she has been lately.
That's why I'm trying to tread lightly with this
situation. I want to believe she would be happy to
know her long lost son wants to meet her, but you
just never know." Jacoby said as everyone agreed.
"Well, when you tell her you found me and she
asks about her dad, tell her he's dead." Jameson said
as everyone's expression changed.
"You think she's going to ask about our
grandfather?" Jacoby asked.
"Yes, I do. I think that's going to be one of the
first things she wants to know and she may even
panic a little, but if you tell her he's not alive, it will
calm her down because she'll know he can't hurt her
anymore." Jameson said as Jacoby nodded.
"Based on what you've told us so far, that
makes a lot of sense so I'll go with that when she
asks." Jacoby replied.

"You said you still have more to tell us? What is it?" Jarrell asked, anxiously.

Jameson began to tell them the other things that he and Cole talked about concerning how his biological father died, the molestation and even the fact that he learned after Damian passed away that he had been having sex with a teenager from his ministry who he had a son with three years ago. His brothers were just as shocked as he was to hear of such things happening among a church and people that were supposed to love God and love God's people. But it made Jameson feel good when Jamaal, Jameson, and Jarrell said how seeing him teach and share today on campus gives them hope to believe that not all pastors are bad people and there are some like him who will treat people right and not mislead them. That meant a lot coming from them because they haven't given their lives to God, and hearing it made Jameson believe that his light was already starting to shine in a way he didn't expect. Jamaal drove Jameson back to his house around nine that evening, and after Jameson called to check on his children and arrange a time to come to Bobby and Crystal's house, he went to sleep. Bobby was getting ready to go out of town for a few days on business and Crystal said they would be alone when they spoke, which made Jameson feel better about the conversation he sensed was about to take place once he got there.

The next morning, when Jameson got up and after eating breakfast, he decided to look up some information for something he wanted to do at his church since he wasn't going to Bobby and Crystal's home until later on today. Jameson wanted to get teaching about the prophetic started as soon as possible now that he sees the major and vital roles that it plays in the Kingdom of God. He didn't want to deprive his ministry of it any longer, especially if there were gifts within his ministry that were waiting to be stirred up in this area. Carlos sent Jameson information about two young prophets from Atlanta named Miranda & Mackenzie Bronson, who are both identical twin sisters. Carlos said they're known for their operation in the prophetic as well as teaching other millennial leaders how to introduce the prophetic to their church and operate in it effectively. Jameson looked up their information and in addition to finding their social media accounts, he found their ministry website and saw that they serve at their uncle's church in Atlanta. Jameson loved that their ministry was very diverse and not limited to just one race. When he saw that Miranda and Mackenzie's uncle was white, he knew that they were mixed race by their fair skinned complexion. He read their biography and saw that they had been in Atlanta since they were babies but were both originally born in Chicago, Illinois just like him to their mother, Amanda Bronson who unfortunately died when they were 2-years-old after being murdered.

Jameson was blown away even more when he realized the twins were the exact same age as him and were born seven days before he was at the same hospital in Chicago. Seeing how much they had in common made him want to connect with them even more, so he reached out to their uncle, Pastor Garrett Bronson, Sr. at the number that was listed to speak with him about his interest in having Miranda and Mackenzie do a teaching at his church. Garrett was very pleasant on the phone and Jameson could tell he was sincere and that he cared about the people he leads just like he does.

Even though Garrett was much older than Jameson, they really connected and Jameson could see himself working with his ministry more in the near future. When Garrett and Jameson began to discuss a time for Miranda and Mackenzie to come to his church, Garrett looked at their calendar and realized that Mackenzie and Miranda had just received a cancellation for an engagement they had in Gainesville two weeks from now. Garrett asked if that time frame was too soon to have them come to his church and with excitement, Jameson told him that time would be perfect before confirming the exact dates. After finishing his call with Garrett, Jameson took a shower and got ready to head over to meet with Crystal and pick up his children who had been staying with them since yesterday morning. Jameson was anxious to see what it was she wanted to talk to him about and could tell by her tone of voice on the phone when he called her again last night that it was really important. On the drive there, Jameson called Alexis to check on her and see how her business trip was going. When Jameson asked what had been going on with him, he almost didn't know what to say. But it was at that moment that

Jameson heard God speak to him and say that it was now okay for him to tell her what had been happening with him lately.

Jameson was excited because he really wanted to bring his wife up to speed on what he was learning about his family's history, but he wanted to wait until they were together and could speak face to face. So, Jameson decided to generalize everything and promised to give Alexis the rest of the details when she got home. Moments after wrapping up his phone call with his wife, he arrived at Bobby and Crystal's home. Bobby had already left for his trip, so Jameson decided to park in the driveway behind Crystal's Red Mercedes Benz. As Jameson got out of his truck, Crystal came to the door as Isaiah, Destiny and Victoria started calling out to him and running to hug and greet him as if they had not seen him in several days. Jameson loved his children very much and seeing the joy on their face when he would come around always did his heart some good. Jameson greeted and talked to each of his children as the four of them walked up the driveway and headed inside the house. Jameson took them down the hall to their play area before coming back into the living room to speak to Crystal who was sitting on the sofa looking at her phone.

"Hey Mom, I'm sorry about that. The kids act like they haven't seen me in forever." Jameson said as she smiled and they hugged each other.

"You don't have to ever apologize to me for loving your children! Yeah, they kept asking when you were coming to pick them up, especially Isaiah. I don't think they're used to you being as busy as you have been lately." Crystal said as they sat next to each other on the sofa.

"Yeah, things have been so crazy lately with the church and people wanting me to help them get resources for their members." Jameson said.

"Yes Jameson, I'm proud of you! You're doing a good thing!" Crystal said as Jameson smiled.

"I appreciate that, Mom. Thank you so much! Mom, you don't think I'm neglecting my kids do you?" Jameson asked, concerned about how his children have been adapting to his busy schedule.

"Of course not! You and Alexis are doing a great job with your children, in spite of your busy schedule. It's funny, Alexis asked me the same thing when we spoke yesterday." Crystal said.

"She did? Yeah, I spoke to her for a few minutes on the way here. I have so much to tell her when she gets back." Jameson said.

"That's good to hear. I still can't believe you found your mom through her sons, that is so exciting to hear. How do you feel?" Crystal asked.

"I feel good. I mean, my brothers are amazing and we spent half the night talking and getting to know one another at Jacoby's house. He actually doesn't stay far from here." Jameson said.

"That's great, Jameson. I'm happy for you. So, you haven't talked to your mom or met her yet?" Crystal asked.

"Not yet. Jacoby is going to let me know when the time is right because of her present condition.

She battles with mental illness and it's pretty bad from what they told me." Jameson said as Crystal nodded.

"Well, you've been helping so many in that area, maybe you will be able to help your mom too." Crystal replied.

"I hope so. But, enough about me, what did you want to talk to me about?" Jameson asked in a concerned tone as Crystal took a deep breath.

"Jameson, I need you to promise me before I say anything, that you won't tell Bobby or Alexis what I'm about to share. I wasn't supposed to say anything about this and Bobby would kill me if he knew I told you. Alexis doesn't know anything, that's why you can't tell her either." Crystal said as Jameson looked confused.

"You can trust me, Mom. I won't tell. What's going on?" Jameson asked.

"It's about the year Bobby got stabbed." Crystal replied.

"What about it?" Jameson asked as Crystal paused for a moment before responding.

"We know who it was that stabbed Bobby, we've always known." Crystal said as Jameson nodded.

"My grandfather did it. That's what you're about to say, right?" Jameson asked as Crystal looked surprised and reacted to Jameson's response.

"Oh my God! Jameson, you knew this whole time? How?" Crystal asked, still in shock.

"I found out a little over a month ago from Pastor Scott before he died." Jameson said as Crystal reacted again.

"Died? Did you just say Cole died?" Crystal asked, surprised.

"Oh, I'm sorry, I thought you and Dad knew. Cole committed suicide. No one told you?" Jameson asked, surprised that Bobby and Crystal weren't aware of his passing.

"No, we didn't know that. Bobby has been trying to reach Cole for weeks and he was literally about to have a breakdown about it because he couldn't reach him. He kept saying he needed some information that I guess Cole was supposed to bring to him, but never did." Crystal said.

"Did he tell you what the information was?" Jameson asked.

"No, he wouldn't tell me and it was freaking me out a bit. But back up for a minute, Cole told you that your grandfather stabbed Bobby? Why?" Crystal asked, still in shock.

"I guess you can say we sort of beat it out of him." Jameson replied.

"You said "we." You weren't alone when this happened?" Crystal asked.

"No, Ethan and Nick were with me too." Jameson said as Crystal shook her head.

"Oh my God! He told all three of you? Why? I"m not understanding. I didn't even know you were still in contact with Pastor Scott after he got angry and left the church." Crystal said.

"I wasn't. I ran into Pastor Scott at Grandpa's storage unit. I went there because I was looking for something I needed and I was hoping to find it in his old stuff. There's a lot of stuff in there so I asked Nick and Ethan to meet me at the unit the day I went." Jameson said.

"Okay, I understand that part, but how did you end up talking to Cole?" Crystal asked.

"We were inside the unit looking through my grandfather's stuff and Pastor Scott showed up. He didn't expect to see us and panicked. He then tried to leave and pretend like he came to the wrong unit by mistake, but I knew that wasn't the case so we ran after him." Jameson said.

"You beat him up?" Crystal asked.

"No, we didn't beat him up. But we didn't let him leave either. I wanted to know why he was showing up at my grandfather's storage unit and I asked him if he had a key. He said he still had the same key my grandfather gave him years ago when he first got the unit. I told him to hand it over and I asked him why he was there." Jameson said.

"Did he tell you?" Crystal asked.

"He tried to say that he was just there to check on my grandfather's things, but I knew that wasn't true either. He knows I'll look out for my grandfather's stuff, so I made him tell me the reason why he came and I had Nick and Ethan get in his face a bit to make him talk." Jameson said as Crystal sighed and shook her head again.

"So, what did he say?" she asked.

"Well, that's when he mentioned Dad. He said Dad sent him to the storage unit to get a file that had some piece of information in it that he needed." Jameson replied.

"So that's how you realized we knew each other from before?" Crystal asked.

"Yeah, that was the start of it. You and Dad never talked to Pastor Scott like that and I couldn't understand when you exchanged numbers and why Dad would be sending him to my grandfather's unit to get anything." Jameson said.

"I'm sorry, Jameson. I'm sorry we didn't tell you the truth, but there's a reason for it." Crystal said.

"I'm not mad at you and I know. Pastor Scott told me how long you had actually known each other and what happened back in the day. I had a much clearer understanding of why you and Dad were so against going to church. My grandfather put you through hell from what he told me, and he basically kicked you out of the church when he learned that you were pregnant with Alexis. So, I got it, and I'm sorry that happened to you." Jameson said as he grabbed Crystal's hand and she nodded as tears fell from her face.

"I appreciate that Jameson, thank you. So, was that all he told you?" she asked as Jameson sighed for a moment and paused before responding.

"No ma'am, that wasn't all. Pastor Scott told me everything, and I do mean everything. I mean, based on what he told me happened with you and Dad leaving when you did, I'm not even sure if you're aware of everything. I can tell you about it when you're ready to hear it, but I know you wanted to talk to me." Jameson said.

"Yeah, I do and I would like to hear what he told you because it may help me make sense of why Bobby has been on edge lately." Crystal said.

"Well, let's take it one step at a time. Pastor Scott told me that Grandpa stabbed Dad out of revenge for how he treated you guys back in the day when you found out you were pregnant. Is that how you see it?" Jameson asked.

"Yeah, for the most part. Our parents turned on us and everything, it was the worst experience ever. We heard talk about Shannon getting pregnant a year after we had Alexis, but we never knew the details. All we were told was that Damian kicked her out of the church, which shocked us. I mean, we didn't think he would kick out his own daughter." Crystal said.

"You came to Gainesville before my grandfather came, right?" Jameson asked.

"Yeah, we came here after we left to attend college here at the University of Florida. I'm not sure if Cole said anything about that or not. I don't even think he knew we were here." Crystal said.

"He didn't know, but Alexis told me what you guys told her about your journey through college and raising a child." Jameson said.

"Yeah, it was hard, but we did it." Crystal said.

"Mom, can I ask you something?" Jameson asked.

"Sure..."

"You keep saying my grandfather stabbed Dad out of revenge. I understand what he did to you, but what did my grandfather think you did to him to make him come after Dad in that way?" Jameson asked as Crystal paused for a moment before responding.

"This is why I'm afraid that you will get upset with me." Crystal said as tears fell from her face again and Jameson became even more confused.

"Why would I get upset with you? Just tell me, Mom. You might as well at this point." Jameson said.

"Bobby found out where your mom was and that she was alive. When he found this out, he confronted Damian about it and called him out for lying about her being dead all these years." Crystal said as Jameson released Crystal's hand and she began to apologize repeatedly.

"You found my mom back then and didn't tell me?" Jameson asked, sternly.

"Yes, and I'm so sorry. We are so sorry, Jameson. But, we did try and that's why Bobby got into it with Damian. See, Damian offered to pay Bobby off to keep him quiet about what he knew. But Bobby didn't want to do that, he threatened to expose Damian by telling you the truth about where your mom was." Crystal said.

"So he threatened my grandfather and my grandfather stabbed him to shut him up? Is that what you're saying?" Jameson asked, surprised.

"Yes, that's exactly what happened." Crystal said.

"Mom, I don't understand. Why didn't you tell the police the truth? I know he's my grandfather and he was the pastor of the church, but he should have gone to jail for what he did! You should have told me you found my mom! You know how hard not knowing anything about her has been for me!" Jameson said as tears fell from his face and Crystal tried to grab his hand and he pulled it back.

"Jameson, I know we were wrong and I'm sorry. I am so sorry." Crystal said, sadly.

"You knew my mom was here in Gainesville all this time and you didn't even tell me. I had to randomly find my long lost brothers to get to her! How could you do that? Weren't you friends with my mom?" Jameson asked.

"Yes, we were and I'm sorry Jameson. I know we were wrong, we just weren't thinking at the time.' Crystal replied.

"Look, I don't know why Dad is panicking right now. But tell him that Cole is dead, so whatever information he was looking for isn't coming from him." Jameson said as he started to get up from his seat and Crystal stopped him.

"Jameson, wait! Please! I'm sorry and I really hope you can find it in your heart to forgive us. We love you." Crystal said, as she cried more.

"Just give me some time, okay?" Jameson asked as Crystal nodded.

"Okay, sure. I'll give you some time." Crystal replied.

"Last thing, is there anything else that you haven't told me that I need to know?" Jameson asked as he glanced over at Crystal.

"Yes, there is one thing." Crystal said.

"Okay, I'm listening. What is it?" Jameson asked.

"Well, let me ask you, did Cole tell you anything about your biological father?" Crystal asked.

"Yeah, he told me his name was Apostle Shawn Anderson and that Grandpa killed him when he found out he had sex with my mom and got her pregnant when she was teenager." Jameson said as Crystal nodded.

"Yes, I heard that too. Is that all he said?" Crystal asked.

"No, he also said that the fallout with him is what brought my grandfather to Florida. He was kicked out of the network they were a part of in order to spare Apostle Anderson's reputation. I don't remember all the details verbatim, but he said Grandpa killed him and made it look like an accident. Did you know that?" Jameson asked.

"No, I never knew your grandfather killed him, but I'm not surprised." Crystal said.

"So, what were you about to say about him?" Jameson asked.

"Covering up his sexual relationship with Shannon wasn't the only reason the network responded the way they did. Around the same time that it came out about Shannon being pregnant with his child, Shawn Anderson and his wife had just found a way to get rid of a woman who was claiming that she was also pregnant with Shawn's baby." Crystal said as Jameson reacted to what she said.

"Are you serious? There was another woman pregnant by him at the same time as my mom?" Jameson asked, surprised.

"Yes, that's what I heard from a source who was in the network at the time. Damian and Cole were gone by then, so he probably didn't know. He never mentioned this, did he?" Crystal asked as Jameson shook his head.

"No, he never mentioned it. You're right, I don't think he knew. Did she keep the baby?" Jameson asked as Crystal nodded.

"Yes, she kept the baby, both of them." Crystal said as Jameson looked surprised.

"Both of them?" he asked.

"Yes, I was told she gave birth to identical twin girls. See, the woman was a white prostitute that ended up sleeping with Shawn one weekend when his wife was out of town for a conference. She got pregnant and showed up at his house shouting it from the mountain tops. Shawn's wife was ready to kill that lady, but the other members who were there held her back and made this woman leave. My source told me that Shawn tried finding her later and offered to pay for her to have an abortion, but she refused." Crystal said.

"So, he let her go?" Jameson asked.

"He had no choice but to let her go. She made sure she wasn't alone when they had their conversation in case he got upset. No one ever saw her again, but my source has eyes everywhere." Crystal said.

"Who's your source?" Jameson asked.

"I can't tell you that, just know it's credible." Crystal said.

"So I have twin sisters the same age as me?" Jameson asked, surprised.

"Yes..."

"So did your source tell you this woman's name? Does she know her daughters' names or what happened to them?" Jameson asked.

"The woman's name was Amanda Bronson and her daughters' names are Miranda & Mackenzie Bronson. Amanda gave her daughters away to their uncle, which is her brother and I was later told that Amanda was killed by some guy she was dating six months later when the girls were still infants." Crystal said as Jameson reacted to what she said before getting up and pacing the floor. "What is it?"

"Did you say Miranda and Mackenzie Bronson?" Jameson asked.

"Yeah, why?" Crystal asked.

"Mom, they're getting ready to come teach at my church in a couple of weeks! Look! Is this who you're talking about?" Jameson asked, showing Crystal a picture of them on their website.

"I never met them before, Jameson, but that's probably them." Crystal said.

"Their bio said they were born in Chicago, but they've been living in Atlanta with their uncle, Garrett Bronson, who's a pastor." Jameson said as Crystal nodded.

"That makes sense. My source said that Amanda's brother was a preacher from Atlanta, but she never said his name. So yeah, Jameson, these are your half-sisters and you're the same age. I think they were born ahead of you, but not by much." Crystal said.

"Oh my God, I can't believe this! I can't believe this!" Jameson told her, still shocked at the news. "I need to call their uncle back and tell him. I mean, that's okay, right?"

"Yes, of course you can, Jameson." Crystal said as Jameson nodded.

"I'm going to get the kids and head home. Thanks again for watching them. Are you sure that's all you needed to tell me?" Jameson asked, glancing at her sitting on the sofa drying her face with tissue.

"Yes, that was all. I was worried about Bobby doing something crazy to Cole for not calling him back, but I can see we have nothing to worry about now." Crystal said as Jameson nodded before walking to the playroom to get his children ready to leave.

Even though Jameson was still upset with Crystal for not telling him that she and Bobby knew where his mom was, he still gave her a hug before leaving to take Isaiah, Destiny and Victoria home to take their afternoon nap. Jameson drove home in tears the whole time as he thought about everything that he learned after talking to Crystal. The secrets about his family and his journey into this world continued to unfold themselves, and for Jameson, it was a lot to take in. About an hour after Jameson was home and his children were in their rooms sleeping, he received a call from his half-brother, Jacoby, and he had great news that made Jameson very excited.

Jacoby began to tell Jameson that he spoke to their mom and in tears, she said that she was ready to finally meet her long lost son. Jacoby asked Jameson had any time tomorrow to meet him and the rest of their brothers at the facility where Shannon was staying and Jameson immediately agreed to meet them. Because visiting hours on Sundays worked differently than during the week, Jameson's only option was to come around ten in the morning, which is usually the time that they're in service. Jameson quickly reached out to Ethan and Nick about it, and they agreed to cover everything tomorrow while he was gone. Jameson got ready to text Crystal to see if she would watch his children again while he made his visit and before he sent the message, Jameson heard God tell him to ask Ethan and Nick to watch his children while he was at the facility instead of taking them back to their grandparents' home. Jameson was totally caught off guard by what God instructed him to do, but he did listen and he asked Nick and Ethan if they were willing to keep his children with them tomorrow since their children were out of town for the weekend with their moms and wouldn't be back in town until late Sunday afternoon. Nick and Ethan agreed to help him and didn't ask any questions about why he was asking them to watch his children instead of their grandmother.

It was now the moment of truth for Jameson as he arrived at the facility where his mother was staying and waited in the lobby area with Jacoby and the rest of his brothers. A nurse came to let them know they were permitted to see Shannon who had been moved to an area inside the facility where they could talk alone while security stood outside the door. Jameson walked into the room with his brothers as the nurse led them inside, and he saw a tall, slender, brown skinned woman with long, beautiful black hair sitting in her gown and slippers near the window drinking a cup of tea. Jameson stood behind with his brothers as Jacoby walked over to where she was sitting. Jameson then signaled for Jameson to walk over to them so she could see him, and Jameson nervously walked over to them as the rest of his brothers followed.

"Hey Mama, we're here." Jacoby said as Shannon slowly turned her head to him and smiled slightly.

"Hey baby, you made it back to see your mama?" she asked as she and Jacoby hugged each other.

"Yes ma'am, we're back. Look who's here, Mama. Remember, I told you I was going to bring your oldest son, Jameson, to meet you." Jacoby said as he helped Shannon stand up and she faced Jameson for the first time ever.

"Oh my God! Is this my baby? Jameson, is that you?" Shannon asked.

"Yes ma'am, it's me! Hey Mama!" Jameson said as they both started crying and they began hugging each other closely as Jacoby and the rest of his brothers stood around them.

"I can't believe it's you! I really can't believe it's you! I have missed you for so long! I love you so much and I am so sorry! I am so sorry!" Shannon said, crying hysterically.

"It's okay, Mama, I don't blame you! I know everything, so it's okay." Jameson replied to her.

"So, you love me, right?" Shannon asked.

"Yes! Yes, Mama, I love you very much! I always have!" Jameson told her as he kissed her on her cheek before they both sat down on the sofa across from each other holding hands as Jacoby and the rest of his brothers sat on the sofa across from them.

"You're so handsome!" Shannon said as Jameson smiled and laughed a little.

"Thank you, Mama. You're very beautiful too. My daughters look just like you!" Jameson said as Shannon reacted to what he said.

"Oh my God, I have grandchildren?" she asked, excitedly.

"Yes, you do! Here they are!" Jameson replied, showing her pictures on his phone. "That's Isaiah, Destiny and Victoria. The girls are identical twins." Jameson said.

"Oh wow, they are beautiful! Yes, they look so much like me! So Isaiah's named after you, right?" Shannon asked as Jameson nodded.

"Yes ma'am, he is. Jameson Isaiah Montgomery, Jr." Jameson replied as she nodded.

"Will I get to meet my grandchildren one day?" Shannon asked.

"Yes you will, I promise! They're with their godfathers today at my church, but I will bring them to meet you soon!" Jameson told her as she smiled and nodded.

"You said you know everything. Damian really told you the truth before he died?" Shannon asked as Jameson shook his head.

"No Mama, unfortunately, Grandpa wasn't totally honest with me before he died and I've continued to find that out since he passed away. I'm curious though, Mama, how did you know he died? I mean, his death wasn't in the paper or anything." Jameson said.

"I paid for a private investigator to locate you and when he found you, he told me that you and Damian were here in Gainesville." Shannon said.

"Wow, you hired someone to find me? How old was when that happened?" Jameson asked.

"You were 2-years-old at the time and so cute! He took pictures to show me, and I wanted to come get you then, even if it meant taking my own father to court. But I was afraid, I was afraid of what he might do to me if he knew I was here and if I tried getting custody." Shannon said as Javon handed Shannon and Jameson tissue.

"So, did you pay the investigator to watch me all these years?" Jameson asked.

"No, I used the information he gave me to keep tabs on you myself. So, in a way, I've watched you grow up. But I had to watch you from a distance." Shannon said as Jameson nodded.

"I understand..."

"You said you know everything, right? If Damian didn't tell you the truth, then how do you know?" Shannon asked.

"Pastor Cole Scott told me everything a little over a month ago. I had a feeling there was more to what Grandpa told me, but I had no idea how much he left out and how much he lied to me until Pastor Scott told me what he knew." Jameson said as Shannon nodded.

"What about Bobby and Crystal? I mean, you've been married to Alexis all this time, they didn't tell you anything?" Shannon asked, surprised.

"Wow Mama, you really have been watching me haven't you?" Jameson asked as Shannon started laughing.

"Yes baby, I have. I've been watching. I was blown away when I realized Alexis was Bobby and Crystal's daughter. I mean, we all grew up together and they had Alexis the year before you were born. I mean, the truth didn't come out when Damian realized he knew Alexis' parents?" Shannon asked as Jameson shook his head.

"Mom, Bobby and Crystal have lied to me too all these years. Crystal just told me yesterday that she's known your whereabouts for the last few years. She tried to confess to her and Bobby knowing my grandfather from back in the day, but like I said, Cole told me everything and he told me all about that!" Jameson said as Shannon shook her head.

"Do you mind telling me everything Cole told you before I start talking?" Shannon asked.

Jameson began sharing the details he knew from what Cole shared with him, Nick and Ethan that day at the storage unit. At certain moments, Shannon became emotional as she nodded in agreement with what Jameson was telling her. It assured Jameson once again that Cole really did tell him the truth and he didn't hold out on him like others had. Jameson told his mom everything including the news about Damian leaving behind a 3-year-old son that he had named after him, and it made Shannon cry even more. Jameson wasn't sure if he was going to share that part with her after learning from Cole that Damian never really wanted daughters but sons, but he felt she had the right to know the truth about having a little brother, even at her age. Jameson and his brothers could tell after he finished telling Shannon everything he knew that it was a lot for her to take in. Jacoby went to get her some more water and some fruit for her to eat before they continued their conversation.

"Oh no, do we have to leave already?" Jamaal asked, as he glanced over and saw one of the nurses walking over to where they were sitting.

"No Jamaal, you're fine. I'm just passing through and making sure Shannon is doing okay, and wasn't in need of anything." the nurse told them as they smiled and nodded.

"Thanks for coming by, I just gave her some more water and fruit from the fridge. That was okay, right?" Jacoby asked.

"Yes, that was fine! Thank you for doing it. Are you feeling okay, Shannon?" she asked.

"Yes, Lacey, I'm okay. Thank you. Look Lacy, remember I told you I had another son? This is my other son, Jameson Montgomery." Shannon said proudly as Jameson and Lacey shook hands.

"Nice to meet you." Jameson said.

"It's very nice to meet you as well, Pastor Jameson! It's an honor!" Lacey said as Jameson reacted to the fact that Lacey knew he was a pastor.

"Oh wow, how did you know I was a pastor?" Jameson asked, surprised.

"Well, you've been the buzz around the city ever since you started encouraging the church to take mental health seriously and doing the teachings and seminars at your church and other places. You're everywhere now!" Lacey said, smiling.

"Wow, that's amazing! Well, thank you for your feedback and for your support, I appreciate it." Jameson said.

"You're welcome, Pastor Montgomery!" Lacey said.

"Visiting hours are over in another half-hour, right?" Shannon asked, sadly.

"Well, that's usually true, but not today. When Jacoby came to add you to the list of visitors, the director saw your name and was blown away. He had no idea you were his mother and Jacoby told him some of your story about being separated from your son when he was born, and wanting to reunite after all these years! So, he told us to let you spend as much time as you need to today. That's why we had you come here instead of the usual meeting area." Lacey said as Shannon, Jameson and the rest of his brothers became excited.

"I had no idea, wow! Thank you so much, Lacey. I'll have to tell him thank you when I see him later." Shannon said, graciously.

"Not a problem, it's our pleasure! Enjoy your time and I'll be back in a bit to check on you again." Lacey said as she waved and exited the room they were in.

"Wow, the director has never been this lenient before. This means so much to me." Shannon said as everyone agreed with her.

"This means a lot to me too, Mom. I am so glad I've finally had the chance to meet you." Jameson said.

"I'm happy to meet you too, Jameson. I am so proud of everything you've accomplished, you've truly made me proud and you've been an inspiration to your brothers even though you didn't know each other." Shannon said.

"I have?" he asked.

"Yes, you have. Why do you think your brothers got into college? I knew you went to college and I pushed them to do the same. I started with

Jacoby because he was the next oldest and I wanted him to set the example for the rest of his brothers." Shannon said.

"I appreciate that, Mama. That means a lot. Can I ask you something?" Jameson asked.

"You can ask me anything!" Shannon said.

"My brothers knew they had an older brother, but they didn't know who I was until they heard me share my testimony on campus this week. How come you didn't tell them who I was and that I was in the same city all this time?" Jameson asked as Shannon sighed and paused for a moment before responding.

"I knew that if I told your brothers who you were and where to find you, they would have come looking for you, even if I would have told them not to. I wanted you to meet and I wanted to meet you too, but it had to happen at the right time. I know this will sound bad but honestly, I was waiting for Damian to die so I could feel safe enough to come for you and bring your brothers as well. I hope you can understand that." Shannon said as Jameson nodded.

"Yes, I understand completely, and I'm sorry you felt the need to do that because of what Grandpa put you all through." Jameson said.

"Thank you for understanding, Jameson. I won't elaborate too much on that, I know that was still your grandfather and that's the only parent you knew growing up." Shannon said as Jameson nodded.

"Yeah, it was. I'm not saying I don't appreciate Grandpa for taking care of me the way he did, but he lied to me about a lot and just from Cole's account, he did a lot of bad things, a lot of illegal things." Jameson said.

"Yeah, he did, and he had been believing all those years that he was untouchable because he was a pastor. Damian, your biological father, Shawn and so many other preachers at that time carried these powerful and influential titles as leaders in the church, but they didn't have the character to back it up. Do you know what I mean?" Shannon asked, sternly.

"Yes ma'am, I understand completely." Jameson said.

"No offense to you, Jameson. Even though I turned away from the church and God years ago, I still support what you're doing. You turned around what was a sinking ship when your father and Cole were running things. If God was going to use someone, he had to use someone who would do right by his people." Shannon said as Jameson nodded.

"Thank you for saying that, Mama. That means a lot. Yes, I do my best to honor God by treating his people right and loving them. Learning everything I did has made me want to do that even more." Jameson said.

"Well, keep going, Jameson. Keep going! If you keep going, the rest of the covers will get pulled back on what's been hidden all these years." Shannon said as Jameson and his brothers glanced at each other.

"What do you mean, Mama?" Jameson asked, concerned as Shannon took another drink of her water before responding.

"I didn't know that it was Damian who killed your father for sleeping with me when I was a teenager and getting me pregnant. It was always said that he died of a heart attack and I thought Damian being kicked out of the network was to cover his butt with getting me and that white prostitute pregnant." Shannon said as Jameson reacted to what she said.

"Mom, wait! I was going to ask a little later, but you're talking about Amanda Bronson, right?" Jameson asked as Shannon looked surprised.

"Yes, I am. How did you know her name? I know Cole never knew it." Shannon said.

"You're right, he didn't know it, but Crystal knew her name. She mentioned it when we spoke yesterday." Jameson said.

"How did Crystal know her name? Did she say that?" Shannon asked.

"Crystal kept saying it was a source who told her all of this, but she never said who." Jameson said as Shannon nodded.

"Well, knowing Crystal, that could be anyone. But yes, that was her name." Shannon said.

"Mom, I found her daughters. They're licensed ministers at their uncle's church in Atlanta, and they're actually getting ready to come speak at my church in a couple of weeks." Jameson said as Shannon reacted to what he said.

"Are you serious? So, you've connected?" Shannon asked.

"Well, we did, but they don't know I'm their half-brother yet. See, I didn't find out everything until after I scheduled for them to come." Jameson said.

"Oh wow, so they're in the church too? I guess that's good to know after the lifestyle their mom lived. But I need to tell you something about that, Jameson. But don't tell them or their uncle this because they may not believe it and since Shawn is dead, there's nothing that could be done anyway." Shannon said.

"Sure, Mama, I won't tell them. What is it?" Jameson asked, concerned.

"You said Cole told you that Amanda Bronson was killed by some guy she was messing with, right?" Shannon asked.

"Yes, that's what he said. That's not true?" Jameson asked as Shannon shook her head.

"No, that's not the truth and the fact that Cole didn't know what really went down is proof that Shawn really covered his butt. Jameson, Shawn had Amanda killed. He paid someone he knew in the streets to kill her. But with her being a prostitute, no one cared like that when she died. They just assumed she was murdered by one of her clients." Shannon said as Jameson looked surprised.

"Mama, are you serious? He had her killed? Why? Was she going to expose him or something?" Jameson asked.

"Yeah, she was. My source said she had already given her girls to her brother so he could raise them and keep them safe. But she still wanted to expose him for the liar and deceiver that he was. A lot of people didn't know this but Amanda was trying to get off the streets at that time." Shannon said.

"She was?" Jameson asked.

"Yeah, she was and so were a few other women like her. Shawn promoted a program at his church designed to help prostitutes and women who had been victims of sex trafficking get help and get back on their feet. But it turned out to be nothing more than a ploy to get loose women close to them. The women just ended up getting used for sex in the end." Shannon said as Jameson sat and thought for a moment.

"So wait, are those the women Shawn, Grandpa, Pastor Scott, and those other leaders were having sex with in their church?" Jameson asked, disgusted as Shannon nodded.

"Yeah, it was them. Cole was probably too ashamed to say that part, but it was them. That's why Damian freaked out the way he did when he found out Shawn was messing with me. But Shawn was jealous of Damian, always had been. They were trying to act like they were friends, but they were never friends." Shannon said as Jameson shook his head in disbelief.

"So, Shawn killed Amanda to keep her quiet and then Grandpa ended up killing him for what he did to you?" Jameson asked.

"That among other things. I mean Damian didn't care about me or my sisters because he wanted boys. I was already gone when this happened but

Damian was right. My dad's temper went through the roof after he found out the doctor made a mistake with my twin sisters and told him he was having two boys. She feared for their lives because his hatred had gone to another level." Shannon said.

"That is messed up, and I wanted to ask you about that. Have you seen or spoken to your mom or your sisters at all since you left? Cole told me what he could and I found this picture in Grandpa's stuff." Jameson said as he showed Shannon and tears fell from her face.

"No, I haven't seen them, but I wish I had found the courage to seek them out sooner. They had been living in North Carolina all these years. I had the investigator track them down for me too." Shannon said.

"Wow, that's where they are? They're living there today?" Jameson asked.

"All of them are there except for our mother. She's not alive anymore." Shannon said as she started crying and Jameson took her by the hands.

"Mama, I am so sorry. I'm sorry you didn't get that chance to see her again before she passed away. Do you know how she died?" Jameson asked as Shannon nodded.

"She was battling mental illness just like that, but I don't know if she was being treated for it or not. She killed herself four years ago now." Shannon said as Shannon and his brothers reacted to what she said.

"Oh no, Mama. I am so sorry to hear that. Has she always been battling with mental illness?" Jameson asked.

"If she was, she hid it. That's what they teach you to do in church, hide what you're going through. That's why what you're doing is such a big deal because the black church we know never talks about stuff like this. Maybe if we would have, more people would be alive and we could have healed better." Shannon said as Jameson nodded.

"So, she suffered in silence because of the reputation as a pastor's wife, right?" Jameson asked.

"Yeah, and she was a preacher too. Your grandmother was a prophet." Shannon said as Jameson reacted to what she told him.

"Grandma was a prophet? Are you serious?" Jameson asked, surprised as Shannon nodded and took another sip of her water.

"Yeah, she was, but she had to hide it because the prophetic wasn't embraced by the church like that at the time, and Damian was never for it." Shannon said.

"Do you know why that was? I mean, Grandpa didn't allow it when he was alive and I honestly didn't give it much thought until I realized I was called to it." Jameson said.

"Really?" Shannon asked.

"Yeah, when I was on campus ministering to students, I suddenly started to prophesy. The reason I invited Miranda and Mackenzie to my church is to teach us about the prophetic and how to introduce it

to the church in a way that's not mystical in any way."
Jameson said.

"So Miranda and Mackenzie are prophets
too?" Shannon asked, surprised as Jameson nodded.

"Yes, they are, and I heard a lot of good things
about them too." Jameson replied.

"I don't really know why the prophetic wasn't
embraced during that time, it was just a standard
among the network." Shannon said.

"If Grandma had to hide her gift as a prophet,
how did you know she was one?" Jameson asked as
Shannon paused for a moment before responding.

"I overheard your grandmother on the phone
one day talking to a friend of hers who was a pastor's
wife in Memphis. Their church believed and operated
in the prophetic heavily. So, when my mom was
feeling down about hiding her gift, she would talk to
her about it and one time I overheard their
conversation. That's who I figured it out. Her friend at
the time was telling her that she was free to come to
their ministry so she could flow in her gift. I think my
mom wanted to do it, but she knew what kind of
problems it would start if anyone Damian knew saw
her there, so she never did it. But she wanted to."
Shannon said as Jameson nodded.

"Wow, so in a way, I'm doing what she never
did. I'm carrying her torch!" Jamesons said, excitedly.

"Yeah, that's one way to look at it. Listen,
Jameson, you will probably never see me in church,
ever. If your brothers want to go, that's up to them.
All I will tell you is that if you're going to lead people,

do it right." Shannon said as Jameson nodded in agreement with her.

"Yes ma'am, I am. I promise." Jameson said as Shannon smiled and kissed Jameson on his forehead. "Can I ask you something else?"

"Of course!"

"How would you feel about going to North Carolina and reuniting with your sisters? They have to be missing you after all these years, especially now that your mom is gone." Jameson said as Shannon paused and thought for a moment before responding.

"You think they want to see me?" Shannon asked as tears fell from her face.

"Yes, Mama, of course they do! I know they miss their big sister." Jameson said to her.

"I just know I wasn't the best example growing up. I did a lot of bad things at my young age. I started having sex with guys in high school and college when I was 12-years-old, and some of them paid me to keep quiet. That's why the whole thing with Shawn wasn't a big deal to me like it was to my parents. I know I let them down." Shannon said, guilty.

"Mom, it's okay. It's really okay, we all make mistakes. I know that your sisters don't hold that over your head now, they miss you! They miss you and if they had the chance to see you, it would change their life like you wouldn't believe." Jameson said.

"We will come with you, Mama." Jacoby added.

"I've had their last known addresses and phone numbers for a while now. I was just too afraid to reach out to them all this time, I didn't know what they would say." Shannon said.

"Okay, I understand. We can take it one step at a time by calling first before we visit, and we can do it together. Would that be okay?" Jameson asked as Shannon smiled a little and nodded.

"Can we start when I go home this week?" Shannon asked.

"We sure can, just let me know when you're ready." Jameson said as he and Shannon hugged each other.

"I love you so much, Jameson." Shannon told him.

"I love you too, Mama. This has been great." Jameson told her.

"Yeah, it has. Jameson, before you get ready to leave, I need to tell you something else. You're going to find out anyway, but I think you should hear it from your mother first." Shannon said as Jameson's expression changed and he glanced at his brothers who were just as confused.

"What's going on?" he asked.

"It's about your grandfather's death. I don't believe he really died of a heart attack, I believe he was murdered, and I suspect it to be one of two people." Shannon said as Jameson reacted to what she told him.

"Mama, are you serious? You think Grandpa was murdered? By who?" Jameson asked, concerned as Shannon sighed.

"I don't know for sure, but you may not believe me when I tell you." Shannon replied.

"Just tell me..."

"I think it was Bobby. Bobby's had it out for Damian since he kicked him and Crystal out of the church for getting pregnant and then later finding out about all the dirt he, Cole and the other preachers were doing behind closed doors. I know Bobby went to medical school and became a doctor, but he really wanted to preach like his dad, and Damian messed all of that up for him by embarrassing him and Crystal the way he did back then. Then Damian stabbed him to keep him from speaking up about finding me alive." Shannon said.

"I can see Bobby holding a grudge, but killing my grandfather, especially when he knew how close we were? There's no way. I mean, all of this was a long time ago! It's not worth killing someone over, especially in the church!" Jameson said.

"Jameson, people are capable of anything when they're not healed, even in the church and especially among leadership! Leader wounds are the worst wounds, and they're the most dangerous!" Shannon said.

"Grandpa said that to me before he died. He said leader wounds were the worst wounds." Jameson said.

"Yeah, he should know. Baby, people have died because of some pain or hurt they couldn't let go of. The cycle keeps repeating itself!" Shannon said.

"What do you mean by that?" Jameson asked.

"I mean, Damian isn't the only one with blood on his hands, it goes back a generation." Shannon said as Jameson looked surprised.

"You mean with Grandpa James?" Jameson asked.

"Yes, I mean your great grandfather, Pastor Jameson *"James"* Montgomery as well as your great grandmother, Ayda. A lot of people didn't know this, but Damian did, he always knew. I'm kind of surprised he still chose to name you after him, but he did." Shannon said.

"What did they do?" Jameson asked, curiously.

"I know Damian probably told you all these great things about your great grandfather, but he only did it because he had spent his entire life trying to be accepted by him and loved in the same way that he saw him love his brother, Ricky." Shannon said.

"Grandpa told me about his brother, Ricky. He's in prison for murdering someone, right?" Jameson asked as Shannon gave a smirk and shook her head a little before responding.

"Wow, is that how Damian put it? Yeah, he went to jail for murder, but there's more to the story." Shannon told him.

"I'm listening..." Jameson said.

"Grandma Ayda had an affair with a man around the time that she got pregnant with Damian. Now of course back then, there were no paternity tests to confirm if James was really Damian's father. Damian was 2-years-old when Grandpa James found out about her affair and he questioned if Damian was really his kid and it had them arguing like crazy, even while running the church." Shannon said.

"Wow, Grandpa never told me that. He always acted like he had a good relationship with his parents, and he said it was why he wanted me named after him." Jameson said, surprised at what his mom was saying.

"Yeah, Damian always liked for things to be something it wasn't, and I know him doing that was his way of not dealing with the pain of having the man he knew was father deny him as his son because of his mother's affair." Shannon said as Jameson nodded.

"So, what happened?" Jameson asked.

"Grandpa James didn't divorce Mama Ayda in order to maintain his reputation as the pastor, but it did nothing to change how bad Damian was feeling watching Ricky be treated differently and much better than he was being treated. Mama Ayda continued her affair and came up with a plan to kill Grandpa James so she wouldn't have to worry about him anymore. She poisoned Grandpa James and he later died of what appeared to be a heart attack. A week after the funeral, Grandma Ayda goes to her lover to say they can be together freely and it caught him off guard and he knew at that moment that she killed her own husband, who was the pastor of the church so they could keep seeing each other." Shannon said.

"Let me guess, it was too much for him to handle so he brushed Grandma Ayda off, right?" Jameson asked.

"You're smart, yes. That's exactly what happened. Grandma Ayda got mad and tried to kill him, guess how she tried." Shannon said.

"What did she do?" he asked.

"She stabbed him in the stomach. She asked if they could talk, he agreed and while they were at his house alone, she stabbed him when he still refused to keep seeing her." Shannon said as Jameson and his brothers reacted to what Shannon told him.

"This is crazy! Wow! So, she went to jail when he told the police?" Jameson asked.

"No, he didn't tell the police it was her. He made it sound like he didn't know because he was afraid of his wife finding out about the affair if he gave them her name, so he kept it to himself. The same way Bobby did when Damian stabbed him based on what you told me." Shannon said.

"I can't believe my ears right now." Jameson said, still in shock.

"There's more!" she said.

"Are you serious?" Jameson asked.

"Yes, there's more and you need to hear it so you will see how the cycle has repeated itself. Grandpa James found out about Grandma Ayda going to see the guy she was having the affair with and he got angry and slammed her head against the wall during a heated argument. She died instantly and they ruled it an accident. Damian got angry because he watched them argue that night and he saw Grandpa James kill his mother, and he wanted revenge when they didn't arrest him." Shannon said.

"Are you about to tell me that Grandpa killed Grandpa James?" Jameson asked as Shannon nodded.

"That's right, he killed him with his own shotgun, right in the heart. The police came, saw what happened and Damian told them that his brother, Ricky killed Grandpa James and Mama Ayda out of rage. Evidence had not evolved, so they had very little to go on, but they believed him." Shannon said.

"So, they took Ricky to jail for murder instead of Damian?" Jameson asked.

"Yeah, they did and Ricky was sentenced to life in prison. I asked the investigator to find out what happened to him and Ricky killed himself in prison after five years and no luck of getting an appeal to overturn his sentence. But it was discovered that Ricky had a son with the girl he was dating back then. She had just learned of her pregnancy when Ricky was arrested.

"You know what? I need to call the detective back and give him his name. His name is Derrick Mongtomery, II and he lives in Atlanta as far as I know. His son, Derrick "Elgin" Montgomery, III is there too and he's your age. If Ricky told Derrick or even Elgin about what really happened to him, I wouldn't be surprised if Derrick or Elgin didn't come to Florida and kill Damian as revenge. Yeah, I better call him about that because Derrick would have more

of a motive to kill Damian than Bobby would!"
Shannon said.

"What detective? You've talked to a
detective?" Jameson asked, surprised.

"Yeah, I did. I called the police department and
asked who was working in homicide at that time and
they told me who it was, but also said that they were
retired and no longer working. I told this detective
what I knew and why it was important that I spoke to
someone who could reopen these cases and solve
these murders that were marked as accidental
deaths. They weren't accidents!" Shannon said,
sternly.

"So, they got you someone?" Jameson asked.

"Yeah, they did, but he lives here in
Gainesville. They had me talk to him because he's the
son of the very detectives working homicide during
that time in Chicago. I spoke to him, and the ball is
rolling because he reviewed the autopsy for Damian
and realized he never died of a heart attack, he was
drugged with an illegal substance from a needle
injection. Detective Pearce is working right now to
look into everything I said and he's even going to call
his father and his grandfather who were both
homicide detectives on the force at those times!"
Shannon said, excitedly.

"Mama, are you serious? There's an active
investigation going on now?" Jameson asked.

"Yes, there is! I know that people like Shawn,
Damian and others have already died, but the truth is
coming out one way or the other and people like me
will finally be vindicated when these leaders are

exposed for the snakes they are!" Shannon said as she started crying and Jameson nodded.

"Wait, did you say Detective Pearce? As in Detective Terry Pearce?" Jameson asked.

"Yeah, you know him?" Shannon asked.

"Oh my God! His wife is a minister at my church, I know him and their children. I had no idea his father and grandfather were detectives in Chicago!" Jameson said, surprised.

"Yes, they were! Like I said, I wanted you to hear it from me first because Detective Pearce plans to talk to you really soon once he finishes up some things on his end." Shannon said.

"So, Bobby won't be a suspect?" Jameson asked.

"I can't promise that, I don't know. But I know he needs to look at Derrick and Elgin along with Bobby. Somebody killed Damian and they're going to pay for it, and in the process, all the secrets and things that were done to people over the years will be exposed once and for all! When you don't deal with your wounds, they will find a way to deal with you." Shannon said.

ANOTHER TWO YEARS LATER

Two years later, and what Jameson believed would bring him the closure he needed has now created more pain for his life. He found his long lost brothers and sisters, he met his birth mother and his aunts, which ultimately helped him feel a level of completeness he never felt before. Jameson wanted to know where he came from and who he came from. He wanted to understand the parts of his life that his grandfather and others chose to keep from him because they thought it was for the best. But now Jameson couldn't help but wonder if she should have left well enough alone and not gone on the search to find his mother, his aunts and unveiling hidden truths that were rooted deep within the four walls of the church causing trauma and pain to so many people. It's been two years since the investigation behind Pastor Damian Montgomery's death was started by Detective Pearce after several statements, testimony and evidence that was provided to him by Jameson's mother, Shannon Mongtomery. After the initial investigation started, it eventually led to the arrest of Dr. Robert "Bobby" Carrington, Sr. and Dr. Derrick Montgomery, III for Damian's murder.

The outcome of the investigation revealed that Bobby tracked Derrick down and together, they came up with a plan to kill Damian. Bobby still held a grudge for how he and his wife, Crystal, were treated when they were once members of his church and Crystal found out she was pregnant. They were kicked out of the church and everyone, including Bobby and Crystal's immediate family, turned against them in order to remain in good standing with

Damian, the church and the other leaders who were a part of the network at the time. Crystal was still hurt by what happened, but it was Bobby who wanted to do whatever it took to make Damian pay and be held responsible for his actions once and for all. But when his initial attempt to expose Damian by introducing Shannon to Jameson as his biological mother failed when Damian stabbed him, Bobby wanted to take his ploy for revenge to the next level by having him killed. But he knew he couldn't do it alone, so he thought about who else would hate Damian enough to want him dead and decided to ask Shannon. Shannon was in support of Damian being killed, but she was afraid to confront her father, even with Bobby's help and decided to make a suggestion instead.

Shannon told Bobby about her uncle, Ricky and how he went to prison after being charged with killing their father, Pastor Jameson *"James"* Montgomery. Because of Ricky's prior record at the time, the police did not properly investigate what happened, but took Damian's word when he gave his statement saying that Ricky killed their father instead of confessing to killing him himself.

Shannon went on to explain to Bobby that she knew for a fact that Ricky's son, Elgin and his grandson, Derrick were both still very angry about what took place because they were never able to get the charges overturned for Ricky before he eventually died in prison after killing himself. Shannon suggested that Bobby reach out to them to see if they were willing to work together to take Damian out once and for all, and he did. Bobby realized that he already knew Elgin and Derrick by way of them also being doctors in Atlanta and seeing them at a few conferences. It wasn't until his conversation with Shannon that he realized that they were related to each other. Elgin wanted no involvement in killing Damian whatsoever when Bobby first presented it to him and Derrick. He was angry with Damian, but not angry enough to risk his career by murdering him. Bobby was going to come up with his own plan assuming that neither Elgin nor Derrick wanted to get involved, but that soon changed within a week when Derrick reached out to him and said he wanted to get revenge for his grandfather, Ricky by helping him kill Damian for what he did.

They followed through with their plan by killing Damian and making it look like an accident to keep the police from launching a homicide investigation. Derrick and Bobby carried on in their careers without a care in the world because they were certain that there was no way the police would ever find out the truth. That was until Shannon called Bobby and told him that she wanted to talk to a detective and have them investigate the many crimes that had been committed by leaders within the church. Bobby tried getting Shannon to change her mind about it out of fear that having them investigate would lead them to take another look at Damian's autopsy, which was altered by the medical examiner after Bobby and Derrick paid him to make a false report by documenting Damian's death as a heart attack.

When Bobby realized that Shannon was not going to change her mind, he decided to ask her if she would find a way to make sure that the detectives don't take a closer look at Damian's passing in order to make sure that he and Derrick weren't put at risk of losing their careers and being charged. Shannon promised not to mention anything to Detective Pearce about the plan that was created to kill Damian, but that plan fell through during Shannon's interview with Detective Pearce. Shannon accidentally made a statement about Damian's death that was damning and caused Detective Pearce to look at Damian's file once again. After being granted an order from the judge, Damian's body was brought back to the medical examiner's office and another autopsy was completed by a different examiner, who was able to reveal that Damian's heart attack was triggered by an overdose on a narcotic that would typically only be found in hospitals. The high dosage amount counted out the possibility of a suicide and his death was ruled as a homicide.

Once Detective Pearce gathered his evidence, he followed up with Shannon who told him the truth about her knowledge of Damian's premeditated murder by Bobby and Derrick. Her confession and willingness to testify against them in court would keep her from being arrested and charged as an accessory to Damian's murder. Even though Shannon felt bad for throwing Bobby and her cousin, Derrick under the bus, she was more concerned about her own freedom and being able to stay in her sons' lives. Shannon did not tell Bobby or Derrick about her confession to Detective Pearce, but it didn't take long for Bobby and Derrick to figure out who said something to Detective Pearce after they were arrested and taken to jail. The story made headlines in news stations around the world and Jameson learned even more about the many secrets that were being kept from him by those who promised to tell him the truth. Jameson learning about Bobby and Derrick's involvement in Damian's murder shocked him to the core, but he felt the depth of his pain when it was revealed that it was Shannon who helped Bobby come up with a plan with Derrick to kill revenge for all the bad things he had done to many, including leaving his own half-brother to take the wrap for a murder that he committed.

Shannon attempted to apologize to Jameson for her involvement and for not telling him the full truth the day they talked, but Jameson felt betrayed and didn't want to hear anything his mother had to say. Jameson wasn't oblivious to the fact that his grandfather had done some bad things, but Pastor Damian Montgomery would always be the man he saw as more than his grandfather, but his father. Damian was his protection, his provider and then some. He made sure that he had the best life and that he was kept safe, and it was something that Jameson could not overlook even though he knew the truth behind Damian's behavior and everything that led up to and surrounded his decision to raise Jameson on his own.

Jameson's pain grew even deeper when he and Alexis separated and eventually got a divorce as a result of her response to Bobby's arrest and the charges that were against him. Jameson never expected Alexis to stop loving her father, but he was shocked that she sided with him and the rest of her family knowing what he did. Alexis' sister, Kayla was a defense attorney who was planning to represent Bobby and ensure that he be given a light sentence that would result in receiving little to no jail time. The situation tore him and Alexis apart, and he couldn't be with her knowing she was going to support the man who took part in killing the only real father he ever knew in his life.

Nick and Ethan helped Jameson land a good lawyer that allowed him to maintain full custody of his three children and give Alexis weekend visitation. Isaiah was now 7-years-old and seeing his parents apart was taking its toll on him every day because he wanted to see his parents stay together and he couldn't understand the events surrounding their separation. Destiny and Victoria on the other hand, who are now 4-years-old, didn't know what was happening at all. They were just happy any chance they got to spend time with their mother, even if it was only on the weekends. Even though Jameson stopped speaking to his mother, he maintained his close relationship with Jacoby, Jamaal and the rest of his brothers who were still in contact with her. Every now and then, one of them would ask Jameson if he was open to having a conversation with Shannon because she was constantly crying and asking to talk to him, but Jameson refused everytime. Jameson had grown a close bond with his half-sisters, Miranda and Mackenzie as well, and even though they were able to empathize with his pain, they encouraged Jameson any chance they got to talk to his mother and find a way to love her through it with the love of God. But Jameson wasn't trying to hear it and he maintained his position to not speak to her. As a pastor, Jameson knew the importance of forgiveness and not holding a grudge, so he did his best not to hold anything against his mother about what she did even though they were speaking. Jameson continued to preach and lead the people in his ministry, which continued to grow in spite of what was going on. After a long two year wait, Jameson was finally approaching the end of another level of closure he didn't realize he would need as he prepared for the trial that determine the ultimate sentence for Damian's murder.

But, today is another day of unexpected tragedy, tragedy that has now taken its toll on Jameson in a way he could have never imagined. Today he would wear all black on a cloudy Saturday morning as he prepares to bury his mother, Shannon Michele Mongtomery who was unexpectedly murdered inside of her bedroom nearly a week and a half ago. Shannon had been living with Jacoby since her last visit to the behavioral health facility. Jacoby, Jamaal, Javon and Jarrell spent the weekend in Jacksonville for an event with some other friends of theirs and Shannon agreed to stay home by herself while they were gone. Jacoby made sure she had enough food and everything else she would need while they were away, and he promised to check on her daily until they got back. Shannon was doing much better with being to herself, and she didn't have an issue with them being away from her for the weekend. Jacoby checked on Shannon before she went to sleep that Friday night after they arrived in Jacksonville, and by the time he woke up the next morning, he received a phone call from a homicide detective who said they found Shannon deceased inside of her bedroom with more than fifty stab wounds all over her body. Jacoby had an alarm system that did not go off the way it was supposed to because of an unsecured door in the back of the house near the pool that Shannon did not remember to lock before going to sleep that night.

The only reason that the police went to the home was because Jacoby's neighbor from across the street saw someone in dark clothing running away from the house and it made her suspicious. She knew Shannon was home alone and she requested for the local police to conduct a welfare check to make sure Shannon was okay, but the outcome was not what anyone could have expected. The appearance of Shannon's severed body and the amount of blood inside the room was almost too much for the police and detectives to bear as they investigated the scene. Detective Pearce responded to the call thinking that he would now have another murder to investigate when Damian Montgomery's trial was only a month away. But to his surprise, an officer who was checking the perimeter of the house the night of

Shannon's murder found something that would make finding Shannon's killer very easy. The officer found a bloody driver's license just outside the door behind a plant on the ground. After the license had been placed in an evidence bag, Detective Pearce took a closer look and could see that the license belonged to Shannon's uncle, Dr. Derrick *"Elgin"* Montgomery, II. Elgin plotted to kill Shannon for leading police to arresting his son, Derrick for murdering Damian, when it was her idea all along. He didn't think it was fair that she got off without being charged because of her agreement with the police to testify against Derrick and Bobby as well. Elgin wanted to make Shannon suffer the way Derrick was suffering, and he couldn't help but believe that Shannon was just as deceptive as Damian was when he was alive, so in a fit of rage he drove to the house after being given a tip on where she was living from a source he had in Jacksonville and he killed her.

Jameson rode to the funeral with his children sitting next to him and with Nick, Ethan, Miranda and Mackenzie sitting across from him. Jacoby, Jamaal, Javon and Jarrell were in the limousine ahead of them with Shannon's sisters. Jameson rode to the funeral feeling guilty and regretting not listening to Miranda and Mackenzie who kept suggesting that he talk to his mother. They did their best to assure Jameson it wasn't his fault and that he didn't need to feel guilty, but it was easier said than done. All Jameson could remember was his last conversation being a heated one with him leaving and saying that he never wanted to see or talk to her again. Tears fell from his face as

Isaiah sat next to him holding his hand and saying *"Daddy, it's going to be okay."* Jameson kissed Isaiah on his forehead as a way to thank him for doing his best to cheer him up, but Jameson wasn't sure if it was that easy. He really wasn't sure if he would ever be okay again after this. He wasn't sure if he could ever pastor or lead the people he believed the Lord called him to ever again because he was feeling so much pain inside and didn't know where to begin in dealing with it all. Everyone was doing their best to assure Jameson that none of this was his fault, but he couldn't help but wonder if it was his fault.

He couldn't help but wonder if any of this would be happening right now had he just found a way to move on with his life without finding his mother or having that conversation with Cole about the history of his family's dark past.

Jameson thought back to when he was asked if he was ready to find out the truth, and how finding out the truth can sometimes turn out to be more than you bargained for. Jameson understood what was said, but he didn't believe it was possible for that to happen. Finding out where you come from should not create problems, it should serve as a solution and an answer to a question.

Jameson now regrets it all and wishes he could go back to living life with question marks dancing over his head. There wasn't as much confusion back when he didn't know anything outside of what his grandfather chose to share with him. Jameson now sees and is left to deal with the aftermath of leader wounds that never received the healing it needed.

Jameson shook his head realizing that his grandfather was right, leader wounds are the worst. Leader wounds are truly the most dangerous.